# Three Brown Eyed Girls

By

**Rosemary Calabretta**
**Rosaleen Rooney Myers**
**V. G. Wells**

*Cover Photography by Kathleen Myers*

authorHOUSE®

*AuthorHouse™*
*1663 Liberty Drive, Suite 200*
*Bloomington, IN 47403*
*www.authorhouse.com*
*Phone: 1-800-839-8640*

*First published by AuthorHouse     1/12/2009*
*ISBN: 978-1-4389-1578-4 (sc)*

*Library of Congress Control Number: 2008908889*

*Printed in the United States of America*
*Bloomington, Indiana*

*This book is printed on acid-free paper.*

# Three Brown Eyed Girls

All they had were the words. Words gathering like storm clouds in their souls, then spilling through a ray of sun, precious prisms on paper. The depot of each life began at different stations and times, each journey a maze of switches and empty train yards, scattered hopes and misdirection. Fueled by an inner energy they found their way to accomplishment, love, family, but still the storm clouds gathered.

One by one they found themselves together in a creative writing class at a Community College, pens poised, clock ticking, brains in frantic motion looking for the perfect sentence. Then as they listened they found the resonance in each other's stories, stylistically diverse and phrased in bathos, or humor, or anger, reaching across the miles that once separated them.

Celia, a brilliant engineer, a high tech woman with the heart of a poet.

Patsy, a college graduate when she was forty-six, a recovering alcoholic.

Rita, an every woman to everyone, often hiding behind her sarcastic tongue.

And so, they formed a writing group, and the stories grew and they grew in trust and love and courage. They met at Rita's welcoming blue and white kitchen spreading papers and thoughts across the large table, sipping ice tea and munching on caramel coated popcorn. Their voices, as different as their stories, shared the essence of the female experience. One day Celia said, "I think we have the beginnings of a book," and that impetus charged their creative engine.

They needed a title for this potpourri of prose. It was Patsy who said, "We all have brown eyes, why don't we call it *Three Brown Eyed Girls.*" No one thought girls was a silly name to call themselves for despite Rita and Patsy's social security status and Celia's demanding profession, their hearts beat to the freedom of each girl child before her light almost faded in the tunnel of life, and she only had the words.

# Rita

### by: Rosemary Calabretta

# Patsy

### by: Rosaleen Rooney Myers

# Celia

## by: V. G. Wells

# Genesis

# *Out of Place*

There were two trees on 67th Place about halfway down the block. Nestled closely, they seemed to protect each other in an embrace of defiance to the stark cold-water flats, row upon row that flanked them. I wanted a tree. Its regal presence may hide the stoop where Mr. Dobsky sat in his skinny white tee that my mother called his underwear. Its lush, full branches may filter the light on the worn white tiles of the vestibule before the long, dark hallway where a smorgasbord of aromas wafted to the dumbwaiter in the rear. A tree might shadow the front room where I slept next to an upright piano.

The piano was Mom's talisman. Decorated with a lace runner and family pictures, it was a porthole to a cherished past where trees existed in abundance and flowers blossomed and ocean breezes filtered the light. On Sunday afternoons when my New York Grandma and aunts and cousins who lived in Molloy's funeral home on West 23rd Street would come to visit, her fingers flashed tirelessly over the keys. When the plates of cold chicken and ham and cheese sandwiches and sweet pickles were done, the family wended their way through the dark interior rooms, highballs aloft. "Smile the While I Kiss Thee Fond Adieu," "My Wild Irish Rose," were a few of mom's favorites. Grandma, who usually seemed so stern and unapproachable lifted her dress above her knees and danced, revealing her rolled down hose. Someone would eventually ask Daddy to play "Chinatown My Chinatown" which he did with great expertise on the banjo. My brother Georgie and I were always asked to sing and one of our best numbers was "On the Boardwalk at Atlantic City."

They would throw titles at her to play. Mom took a deep breath, hiding any discomfort she'd feel, set her slender figures over the keys and begin. She'd say, "I'll probably hit some bad notes, I don't know that piece very well." In their highball induced glee they didn't care, "Come on, Rose, give it a try." It bothered her, but she covered up, forcing the joy, making the small room where I slept next to the piano a place for pleasant memories.

The shades in the front room were usually drawn, so close to the street on the first floor, it was a condition of privacy, but when the family gathered they were open, letting the music cajole the passers by. The dusky rooms of the flat were connected by mottled interior windows, a feeble invitation to light. In the kitchen the windows faced a small and unkempt yard. I wanted the yard to be nice, to replace the dead weedy dirt with green, but was told that the yard "didn't belong to us." I picture my Mother, sitting by the window, softly moving the white and yellow café curtains. The adjacent yard had a grape arbor, its trellis overhanging a small picnic table where the family gathered in animated conversation. Mom said, "They always seem so happy." It seemed a wistful thought, a reaching in, a touch of melancholy for the home she left in Newport, RI.

God has gifted Newport with a beauty and sense of self that casts an enchanted spell keeping people close in its embrace. Most never leave, and those who do, like my mother, seem haunted in the deep recesses of the soul, perhaps always imagining the morning dew and crisp light on the ocean. Yet, she and my father had tenderness between them, a love that took her away from the home she breathed in her being.

My grandparents, Irish immigrants, came to Newport around the turn of the century, the Gilded Age in Newport. Newport during this time was like a great casino, indulgent and competitive as one by one magnificent estates rose to challenge the beauty of the cliffs, the sea. The Breakers, Marble House, The Elms, Rosecliff, Beechwood stand today as tourist destinations, showing off the excess that was commonplace in high society at the turn of the century. These estates called "cottages" were built by the Vanderbilt's, the Astor's, the railroad and whiskey barons and were the primary employers of the residents. The United States Navy, which has been a presence in Newport since the eighteenth century offered employment at the Torpedo Station, Fort Adams and the Navy Base. In one hundred years our family has grown and prospered, and all but my brother, myself and a handful of second cousins live outside of Newport.

Mom ventured to New York in the 1920's to study nursing at Post Graduate at University Hospital. I do not know why she leapt so far from the tranquil shores to the rambunctious city of speakeasies and flappers and only strangers, but it was brilliant and brave. I do know she embraced her studies, the twelve hour shifts, the tiny room in the nurses quarters where she and her roommate, Samantha slept.

There she met my father, a native New Yorker, born and bred on the east side of Manhattan. Daddy and his east side buddies used to "catch the nurses' eyes," and so they met, as did Mom's best friend, "Sammie" and Daddy's best friend, Eddy Sullivan.

When they were courting they visited Newport with Eddie and Sami and dad's two sisters, Edith and Lolly. They boarded the "Mandalay" at Atlantic Highlands in New Jersey and sailed up the Hudson River to Long Island Sound at 5:00 p.m. as the band played "On the Road to Mandalay." Pictures show them dressed in high nineteen thirties fashion, the women in sleek gowns cut on the bias, the gentlemen in wide lapelled suits. After the revelry the passengers retired to their cabins until the ship docked at dawn in Newport.

Daddy, the New York gentleman, was a handsome man, with auburn hair and green eyes we called "cat's eyes." He became an instant celebrity and eventually a very loved figure in Newport. He had impeccable manners and a gentle nature that belied his "street smart" New York edge. When he would visit in the summers and we would be out and about it seemed he knew everyone in Newport, and as the years passed it became a family joke that he knew more people than Mom.

Some of my earliest memories are of the journey to Newport in the summer. Being New Yorkers we didn't have a car, so we traveled on the New Haven Railroad from Grand Central Station. We waited in the hustle and bustle of the huge rotunda looking at the giant sized

Kodak pictures of travel destinations that circled the station. My brother, Georgie, and I held hands, staying close, listening for the announcement, "Track 3 bound for Boston, all aboard."

The train cars had wicker seats that could be reversed. This was our goal so we could all sit facing each other. Georgie and I hated riding backwards and made sure we were facing the way the train was moving. Mom packed sandwiches and we got an orange drink from the porter. Every few minutes the train stopped on its local journey to Boston, and the conductor came through the train announcing another Connecticut town. As he walked through the cars his voice echoed. "Old Saybrook". "Lyme". "East Lyme". "Westerly". When we heard "Kingston" we knew our journey was nearing an end. Someone from Mom's family, usually Uncle Pat or Uncle Raymond, would meet us at the station, but we still had to negotiate the rural roads to catch the Jamestown Ferry to Newport. Excitement prevailed as we anxiously counted down the minutes to the next ferry. The scent of the honeysuckle, the tingle of salt air heightened the promise of our adventure. It was a wondrous journey across Narragansett Bay, all clear and blue and dotted with outcroppings of small rock islands, or misty and secretive, the foghorn our companion. Georgie and I headed straight for the top deck, and there we stayed till the first bump against the moorings, then another, then the groan and clank as the Jamestown Ferry docked and we were home in Newport for one more summer.

* * *

My great grandfather came to New York in the 1860's and there was a rich family history ground in the dirt and horses' hooves of old New York. When I was a little girl daddy would take me to the city on Sunday afternoons to visit grandma. Her little apartment on 23$^{rd}$ Street was finely decorated with oriental rugs and lovely antiques, a Sheraton secretary, a mahogany butler's table, delicate pieces of cloisonné and English china from my grandfather's antique business, "Ye Olde Curiosity Shop." Prominently displayed on a shelf were two vases carved with monkey figures. It was said the vases turned around when someone was going to die, a rather foreboding tale for a little girl.

Daddy's love of the city was palpable as we walked through the neighborhoods, hand in hand. We'd pass the firehouse that still kept the stables for the horses once used to pull the trucks. I learned if you see a large globe in front of a residence it marks where a former mayor once lived, like Peter Cooper or Jimmy Walker. One day in Greenwich Village he showed me the apartment where Mom had lived on Christopher Street after she graduated, and I thought, "I want to live here on Christopher Street." It had lovely trees. Even then in my child's mind I felt the difference, the excellence of the city and wondered why we lived in a flat in Queens when there was Christopher, or Morton, or 23rd Street where flats opened to a kaleidoscope of excitement. I, like Daddy, was born in Manhattan and felt its gravitational pull in the marrow of my bones.

He worked on Irving Place for Con Edison and his wonderful story telling sense included tales of underground New York. I heard about the first pneumatic subway that ran a block on Astor Place. I heard about the significance of the mosaic designs on the stations, a steamboat at Fulton Street for Robert Fulton, a train at Grand Central Station, a beaver at Astor Place for John Jacob Astor, and the fabulous story of the elephant once lost below the city when it wandered away from the subterranean level of the old Madison Square Garden when the circus was in town. Once in his young life his family had lived above Pete's Saloon near Gramercy Park where O'Henry wrote "The Gift of the Magi," and he showed me the booth, honored with a red velvet rope where the story unfolded. Those walks with Daddy kept me forever enamored of the thunderous glory of New York and resonate like the steady throb of the subways as they pass beneath the streets, nodding to the hundred year old carvings on the platforms echoing the past.

I started first grade the year we moved to Glendale, not yet quite the age of reason, the seven-year-old milestone of first confession and communion. I remembered the apartment we left in Elmhurst, the comfortable rooms, Grandma trying to feed me liver when Mom got sick with pneumonia. I remembered Daddy working two jobs during the war, and the blacked out rooms during air raids. There, on Junction Boulevard I was warm and cocooned. Now, in Glendale I felt chilly and displaced, hated the darkness, the drab linoleum floors, the clanking pipes, the forlorn back yard one could only reach by going through the cold cellar.

The cellar was bounded by bins, each tenant's storage space, and fostered thoughts of evil beings hiding behind the worn wooden slats. The foreboding never left me.

I treasured the New York world. I treasured the Newport world, but my existence in Glendale felt like a shadow world, me a wisp and like my Mom, forcing the joy. As I grew through school and friendship and neighborhood kids I still felt marooned in this place of scurrying things. The kids I grew up with in Glendale were good kids, obedient kids, kids who trembled at the piercing gaze and sweeping gestures of Msgr. Pfeifer, kids who spent every other Saturday in confession, offering their sins of childhood for redemption, suppressing giggles with fear. I was smart and a good student but never felt the shine of me, and seemed to progress through those years as if covered in a silken spider web.

Perhaps the soft silken threads protected me, kept my vision blurred, my memory smudged like the coal bin in the basement or the raging sounds of Mr. Dobsky hitting his wife across the airway. Mom would bless herself, and wring her hands. Daddy would pace. "Something's got to be done about him." But nothing ever was. Interfering was not an option. Mrs. Dobsky was a slip of a woman with downcast eyes and tightly pulled back hair who hurriedly came to and fro, bruised face not quite hidden, mesh string grocery bag close to her chest as she slipped by him on the stoop where he sat in his undershirt with his bucket of beer.

The neighborhood, a mixture of German, Irish and Italian was very clean. It was common to see the hausfraus, their hair covered with a white cap, their sleeves rolled up and aprons in place scrub the pink granite steps of the flats, the big buckets of soapy water flowing down to the street. Mom didn't scrub the stoop. Devoted to her profession and her patients, she was very proud of her Post Graduate cap and told me that all caps were different. Her cap had a black grosgrain ribbon flashed across its starched white peak. And so she would dress in her crisp white uniform, a contrast to her black hair and hazel eyes, her tall lean body straight and proud, her treasured cap in a bag with extra bobbie pins and gently step over the foaming suds, offering a sweet smile and nod of her head.

She learned a way of life perhaps never perceived in her

imagination and ennobled those who she helped, those who sensed a deep spark of passion in her gentle ways. She became friends with the lady upstairs, Mrs. McQueen, an attractive blond who lived alone except when her "special friend" Mr. Schmidt was there. When Mrs. McQueen wanted to see Mom about something she'd clink on the kitchen pipes, or tap on her floor with a broom handle, the Morse Code of the flats.

We did not have a television in those early days, but then not too many people did. The one television in our building belonged to Lorraine Popaduke and on certain days we were allowed to watch Howdy Doody with her little girl.

Like Mom in her crisp white uniform and cap with the slash of black band Lorraine existed in a realm beyond the cold dark halls. She, too, had a piano crammed into her space and her passion filtered through the thin walls in majestic defiance. We were very quiet when she played, absorbing the beauty of Rachmaninoff or Mozart or Beethoven, listening as she'd repeat a phrase over and over again, picturing her long black hair and cropped bangs tossing in the swell of the sounds.

\* \* \*

There are no trees or dappled light softening the stark background in the many photos taken of the family lined up on the steps of the stoop. They chronicle the Easter outfits, first communion, confirmation, graduation, passages of time punctuated against the wrought iron railing, often with a dislodged Venetian blind or the edge of a garbage can tucked in the background. There I am at thirteen in the coat with the velvet collar, my feet turned in a model's stance, my beret at a rakish tilt. My brother, Georgie, all goofy and gangly, and my older cousin, Joseph in an impeccable tweed topcoat are next to me.

Joseph, a few years older than me, was the "brains" of the family on a scholarship to Regis Academy, a prestigious boys school run by the Jesuits. He was born with clubfeet, a potentially paralyzing condition in the thirties, and was taken home by Grandma Rooney, who worked tirelessly on his twisted feet and succeeded. There were always whispers as to why Grandma practically raised Joseph. In retrospect, his mother had three young children. Her eldest, "Chickie," had an enlarged heart and was "slow."

They lived on 23rd Street in Molloy's Funeral Home with their mother, my Aunt Lolly. Their father, Ray Molloy, dropped dead of a heart attack when he was forty-five. "Chickie's" heart gave out when he was twenty-five. Joseph, a special cousin, was gone at fifty-five when his heart stopped too.

They shared this home, a private residence, with the dead. The black and white marble foyer entered into a long hall carpeted in oriental rugs. Softly lighted sconces led up the gleaming mahogany staircase where the bodies were. When we visited we knew to keep our voices quiet past the reception area where the bereaved were being tutored in the business of death. Beyond the hall was the family kitchen and garden. It was there that we usually gathered. It was there that Joseph would point to the back stairs and urge me to creep down to the mortuary, trying and succeeding in scaring his younger cousin. But, the garden was filled with life. French doors opened to a place with swings and wrought iron chairs. I would go there, the sun pelting prisms of light from the surrounding skyscrapers; the sounds of the city muted and feel like a traveler to a secret world.

The family rooms were on the third floor. When the mourners had departed we climbed the long staircase, quietly tiptoeing past the corpses to the living room of gold silk settees, and tasseled drapes.

Aunt Lolly, my father's sister, was a beautiful and flamboyant personality. Her hair had turned white at a young age, and it complimented her aqua eyes. Her feather boas and crystal jewelry lent an air of insouciance to her funeral parlor residence. When she died long after Molloy's had passed into other hands, she was waked there, in bright blue with a feathered neckline. I walked down 23rd Street on that soft spring day, into the foyer and up the staircase, now a mourner. The doors to the kitchen and the back yard were tightly closed.

\* \* \*

My brother Georgie still has friends from the old neighborhood. Now and then he'll tell me, "I saw Bobbie Brodman the other night," and reminisce about roller skating through the linoleum rooms, or playing stoopball with a springy bright pink Spaldeen. But my ties have long since disintegrated, my childhood friends whisked away like crumbs on a rug.

Perhaps Georgie never felt the disconnect of our dual existence, the clan of Glendale kids who'd spend a weekend in Greenwood Lake or go the Schnitzen Park or Rockaway, for we never spent a summer in Glendale. We'd pack up and head to my mother's home in Newport, RI. every June the day after school.

When I was little and my Nana was alive, the house was filled with people, and in my child's eye it seemed like a mansion, but it was only a Cape Cod with four bedrooms that were put to big use. Up the street I go, heart always light as I see the vivid green lawn and beds of flowers so irresistibly inviting. The Newport light is crystalline, the air a delicate nymph. The back door is never locked, open to all who enter and call, "You hoo! anyone here?" The big country kitchen, green and white, has a pot bellied washing machine with a ringer attached and it chirps away. There is a stew cooking on the stove, the white curtains billow in the breeze. As I pass through the pantry I take a gingerbread cookie. The living room is cool, and the easy chairs worn. There is a scent of fresh lemon and stacks of books to read. My four aunts and uncles and my nana Burns live here. How do we all fit, me, my brother, mom and daddy when he comes? I have a comfy bed with a white chenille bedspread. The drawers of the bureau smell musty, but are full of treasures, a music box, hairpins, daintily embroidered handkerchiefs, holy cards, a silver compact. The tree outside the window whispers to the foghorn as I sleep.

I have flashes of memory etched in a groove of perfect happiness; my white pique dress, tanned arms, legs, bare feet; watching the clouds from the roof of Aunt Mary's garage; rain on the porch roof, paper dolls, Mr. Robinson's grape arbor; foghorns at dawn; umbilical cords to the house on Dixon Street. When I wore that piqué dress to Sunday Mass I felt just right, that people could "see me." Perhaps that was the dawning stage of self-consciousness, other awareness, knowledge I was "pretty." It was the only dress I didn't want to take off to go the beach. Mom would say, "Patsy, go change before dinner." I was always very careful of that dress.

When we were home in Glendale a starched pinafore and my neatly tied long brown braids were the objects of derision. I was mocked, especially by the neighborhood brat, Arlene, who wore denim overalls and sneakers. Mom did not approve of little girls wearing overalls. One day I got so mad at Arlene I socked her, and although it was not a ladylike thing to do, I think my parents approved. I didn't feel angry in Newport, and if I was teased it was because of my New York accent, and it was done with affection by the kids whose existence was bounded by Aquidneck Island.

Our days would be spent at the beach, digging for periwinkles, swimming, diving, and always getting sunburned. The ever-present ocean, running barefoot, walking the cliffs in a storm propelled the days of my youth. We dove off cliffs and changed our clothes in the sand dunes. We lay on roofs watching the sunset and imagining pictures in the clouds. We climbed over fences and explored the secret grounds of the many mansions, holding our breath if a groundskeeper came into view. I was the barefoot girl, disdaining shoes for the scratch of barnacles on the cliffs, the tickle of soft dew from the grass, the sand, always the sand, slipping between my toes, the freedom, the joy of just being.

They were glorious days of aunts, uncles, cousins, and other kids visiting grandparents from far off places. Laura and Mary Alice Robinson who lived across the street came from Macon, Georgia and spoke with a southern drawl, a phenomenon in this New England town. Nancy and Eddie Eagan visited their aunt down the street, and this cadre of transplanted New Yorkers and Southerners formed a bond.

The Martins, a family of six kids, lived behind us, and the Fitzgeralds up the street. Tina Martin became a nun, or "took the veil." This was a really big deal. Just the other day looking through old photographs I found one of the group of us and my mother had written, "Tina became a nun." They were the nucleus of our summer friends and we were never lonely.

My birthday in August was always celebrated in Newport, in that other world, and another year passed I was back in school, grade four, then five, then six and no one in Glendale ever shared a birthday with me, until I was sixteen. There are pictures of my "sweet sixteen" birthday party, the cellar strung with lights and garlanded with crepe paper, pink covered tables filled with perfect little sandwiches, coolers with soda and lemonade. I am very pretty in these pictures, my pink faille Jonathan

Logan dress with the square cut neckline a sophisticated promise. It was a dress for class day at my senior year at Dominican, a very special purchase. When I look at those pictures of Valerie, and Ellen, and Mary, Tommy and Bernie and Pat they seemed to be having a good time, a sneaked in beer in Bernie's hand. Mom and Dad gave me this party...in the cellar...for all my friends.

The passage of time had ended the celebration of youth, the prison of the flat a place to escape as I journeyed into the New York world, without my father's hand, negotiating the underground world of subways and tunnels that led to the buildings in the sky. But those days of sweetness clung to me, memories like whispers of sparkle dust that graced my way.

So for fifteen years, as the sun began its slow descent into fall and the chirp of the crickets filled the twilight we knew it would soon be time to leave. As Aunt Alice and Mary and Eileen and my Uncles, Raymond and Pat gave us little treasures for the train, or a dollar bill to tuck in a pocket our tears flooded our little faces. Daddy met us at Grand Central Station and we loaded our luggage into the subway. When we arrived at the bus stop we would take a cab, perhaps to soothe our passage home to the flat, the linoleum floors, the dark halls with the dumbwaiter in the back, and the front room where I slept next to the piano.

# *A Backward Glance*

As soon as I turned onto Hunterdon Street, I knew it was a mistake. I was here in north Jersey, and on a whim decided to visit my old neighborhood in Newark, before heading back to the shore. I pulled up to the three-story house, put the car in park and turned off the ignition. Leaning forward and resting my chin on the steering wheel, I gazed at a building so different from my childhood memory. It looked old and run down, in dire need of paint. The only thing that seemed to have stayed the same was the large crack in the front sidewalk, in which a weed of unknown heredity struggled valiantly to survive in the cement world of the city. The sun beating down mercilessly on the building showed the place to be more derelict than I would have thought.

The Goldes lived on the third floor of 799. *That was us, and it was home until I was almost twelve.* Our place, which was called a railroad apartment because the rooms ran in a straight row, the kitchen in the back, and a short hall with a bathroom off to one side, where if you had to get up during the night to pee, and you turned on the light fast enough, you'd see a cockroach scurry to a crack in the wall. From the hall you entered right into the living room, then a bedroom with no door and another bedroom with a sliding door. My three brothers and I slept in the first tiny room in two bunk beds. I can still feel the scratchy woolen blankets on my cheeks; the ones Daddy brought home from the war, embossed with huge blue letters proclaiming Navy ownership.

I knew what the inside of the building looked like, even after all this time. Up the steps of the stoop and through the door was the stairway leading to a landing. Beneath the stairs was where we would hide or play our childhood games. After the landing came the second floor, another set of stairs and the third floor, where we lived. Whether your doors and windows were closed tight or not, you knew what your neighbors were cooking. The most prevailing odors hung in the hallway; Mrs. Moskowitz was boiling cabbage, Mrs. Kream was doing fish. I loved the times when all you could smell was baking; cakes, cookies, the sweet smell of sugary things. Across from us lived Mrs. Reubin. She would smush her face against the glass door to her apartment whenever someone would knock on our door, trying to see who was there. I'm sure she never realized that everyone was able to see her through the opaque glass.

I glanced to my left, ready to pull away, when I saw a familiar face. It was one of the Parker sisters. They were three girls, not pretty at all, very quiet and shy. Their father was strict and mean; he never allowed them to play with any of us. Dolly was the oldest, then Magda and Cathy, the youngest. They would sit on the porch and watch the other kids play. I remembered the day, coming home from school, I saw Cathy on the porch, crying. I walked over.

"What's the matter, Cath?" I asked. She wasn't used to anyone speaking to her. Surprised, she blurted out that her father was hurting her sisters and her. I don't know why she confided in me that day, but I learned that the man was molesting all his daughters! When she realized what she had done, Cathy begged me not to say anything to anyone or her dad would kill her. Of course, I didn't, and now I wish I had been old enough to know that I should have. I feel ashamed, even now, that I never gave away the awful secret. I was maybe nine at the time.

And here, after so many years, was one of the sisters, sitting on the same porch. I *had* to walk over. "Do you remember me?" I asked. "Sure, I recognized you from across the street. Rita, right?" It turned out to be Magda I was speaking to. After asking about the other girls, there wasn't much to say, for Magda didn't know what Cathy had told me. The woman was the same as when she was young; quiet, unkempt, shabbily dressed.

I put the car in gear, and took one long look around before driving off with mixed feelings; reluctant, yet anxious to leave it all behind. It would never be the same. I pulled away from the curb slowly, remembering the times before we left this place forever...

Every summer was spent at the shore, one full week and then every weekend until school began. It was a treat to leave the city, to get away from the stifling heat of the windless metropolis. While riding in the car with my mother during one of these vacations, all of a sudden she stopped short in front of a large old house on the corner. When we kids stopped bouncing off the seats, we looked around and saw a For Sale sign hanging crookedly on the side of its porch. Mom got out and climbed the stairs to the front door. "Wait in the car," she yelled. After maybe an hour she appeared with papers in her hand. She bought the house!

When my dad came home that weekend, and she told him what she had done, his response was not surprising. "That's good, Sue, when do we move?" Daddy didn't care where we lived, as long as we were all together. He was a long haul truck driver, so he wasn't home during the week.

It was 1950 in Long Branch, New Jersey. Elvis was on his way to becoming 'The King'. Kids were finding their thrill on Fats Domino's Blueberry Hill. A young girl with a long ponytail and intense brown eyes was attending high school here; that would be me. *Being a transplant from Newark, I was having a hard time fitting in.* I was a tough city kid and a tomboy, used to a fast-paced life. The people here made friends easily; in the city you usually had to beat someone up before they became your friend. My attitude stamped me as a rebel. I wanted to be back with my buddies, and made no bones about it.

I thought longingly of my best friend, Annie Mc Donald; Annie with the stringy brown, unwashed hair that looked like she combed it with dirty fingers, if she combed it at all. Annie who showed me how to steal from the corner grocery store, dumping food and sundries down her leggings; nothing bulky, packets of Lipton Noodle soup, loose dinner rolls, and her favorite, Baby Ruth bars; most anything that would fit in those baggy pants with elastic bottoms so the stolen items wouldn't fall out. Her mom was the Artful Dodger. She would tell Annie what she wanted and Annie would go to the store, sans money, and fill the order. Yes, I missed Annie most of all.

And the gang; I missed the gang. I was the youngest member, a member only because my brothers were stuck with me after school while my mother worked. Being a tough little kid, I was allowed to hang with them. All we did was play stick ball, steal from the corner store, and 'protect' our neighborhood. Most city kids didn't have bikes, so we made scooters from orange crates and a slat of wood with a roller skate split and nailed to the bottom of both ends. It got us where we wanted to go!

One year near Christmas, my brothers, Tommy and Junior, corralled the gang to get our baby brother a train set. A really crazy idea- no one had any money! They came up with a master plan; to steal the set, piece by piece. And they set out to do the deed. Each day, a different boy would go downtown to Broad and Market Street, enter Bambergers' and steal a part of the Lionel train the boys had their sights on. They would drag me along, an *innocent* little kid, to divert suspicion from a single boy wandering around the store. Each took his turn on different days over a period of time. Dom stole the engine, Bobby the caboose, Tommy the tracks, Junior the transformer, and Ernie an odd car. They got away with it; Dannyboy had a train set for Christmas.

*Didn't mom wonder where it came from?*

At the shore I was always in trouble; with teachers, other kids, and especially with the principal, Mr. Schumacher, who exclaimed in exasperation that I alone was responsible for giving the school a black eye. Actually I gave Shirley Mackey a black eye for picking on a shy little girl who couldn't or wouldn't fight back. Didn't regret doing it, either; it gave me two weeks off for bad behavior, which I thoroughly enjoyed. Of course my mother wasn't happy about her wayward daughter being expelled, and since she worked the three to eleven shift at Bendix, I had the house to myself. Though I was told to stay in, who was to know if I left? Maybe my brothers, who wouldn't squeal on me, though they were jealous of my 'vacation'. "I'm gonna tell mom on you!" was the usual threat, but I knew they wouldn't. I was saved at least for two weeks, from wearing the ugly green gym suit with the shirred elastic legs that puffed out, making you look like a huge green pumpkin. I didn't even mind the penny loafers, or poodle skirt which *had* to touch the edges of your bobby socks. In the city I would have been the laughing stock of the neighborhood in those clothes. Though I followed the dress code, it still didn't make me any more popular with my peers. I didn't let people into my private space, so no one saw the insecure young girl within.

It was also a time when 'good' girls didn't have sex at the drop of a hat, though raging hormones tempted some frustrated teens to do the dirty deed anyway. I felt bad for Diane Dey when the pretty blonde cheerleader got pregnant and was whisked away by her shamed parents, not to be seen again until the following spring, flat-bellied with empty arms. I myself refused to play 'back seat bingo' with boys; I was still waiting for Tony Santos to realize that he loved me. On my first day in the new school, I entered the classroom and spotted this handsome, dark-eyed, Italian boy. I said to myself *"I'm going to marry that boy!"* It took awhile.

The cellar in the new house was dark and unfriendly. The first time I went down there, I thought, *At least there are no coal bins down here.* There were coal bins in Newark, each tenant had their own little hidey-hole; and spooky, shadowy shapes floated around the basement, caused by the one bare light hanging in the center. A terrible flashback came over me; I was eight years old and Mom sent me down the cellar for something. Eddie Moskowitz cornered me there. He popped up in front of me and exposed himself. To my horror he began masturbating. I stood there fascinated and repulsed at the same time, wanting to run away, but glued to the spot. I never told anyone.

Miss Tilly was my English teacher, a prissy old maid with tight, kinky brown hair and a snide way of insulting her students. Once she told a black girl that she was being "niggardly," knowing full well the child didn't know the meaning of the word; she started to cry. I even had to look up the meaning. When I got the chance, I imitated Miss Tilly's New England accent and gave a class report that sort of went… "When I visited Chiner I missed my home in Alabammer. I couldn't find a banananer in all of Chiner." Miss Tilly turned purple with rage, and it got me another visit to the principal. Another black eye!

The older boys in school drag raced. After school they would meet on Hope Road, a desolate area. They would race to see who was 'chicken' and brake before they reached the highway. Buster Antonio's dad had given him a brand new Pontiac convertible and he couldn't wait to drag with it. Since he needed a licensed driver with him, Phylis Worley offered. The whole affair was so stupid in my eyes, but that day I went along with my friend Gracie. I was sorry I did. Buster lost control of the car and crashed. The convertible unhinged, he was thrown from the car, breaking every bone in his body. He died instantly. Phylis was lucky, she lived; with a fractured pelvis and two broken legs. Buster's dad went kind of crazy and nailed Buster's shoes to the floor of his Cadillac. He would cry every time he got into the car. I didn't believe the boys would race after the tragedy, but they did.

Chemistry was one of my favorite classes. Not because I was interested in it, but I would turn the gas jets on and smell up the whole floor, so everyone on the second floor had to run outside until the stink cleared. The students loved it! And of course the rebel was the only person who dared do this. Another visit to the office; another black eye. I remember being blamed for things I didn't do. My reputation preceded me. *I bet the kids in Newark would be proud!!*

I remembered the time in the city when my brother Tommy and I broke into the elementary school on Peshine Avenue, and stole a wagon full of building blocks. One of the basement windows was open so we climbed in and decided to take the wagon as proof of our escapade. We were halfway home when we realized we couldn't take the thing home; how would we explain it to our parents? We couldn't hide it; it was a wagon, for Pete's sake! So we turned around and brought it back. The sad part was that nobody believed what we did. With no visual proof our story lay dead in the water.

My stealing days ended when we moved to the shore. There was no badge of courage for thievery here. But mischief thrived in this girl's heart! If I had a partner in crime it would have been double your trouble, double your fun. And I was lucky enough to find one – Jeannie. We called her Peanut because she was so short. One day we both wore roller skates to school. No one noticed in the classroom, and changing classes was so noisy, no one heard the sound of the skates in the halls. The problem was, a teacher called on Jeannie, who forgot she was on skates, stood up and promptly fell on her ass. Panicked, she looked right at me. The teacher put her hand to her forehead in a 'I should have known' gesture and sent us both to the office. Another black eye.

*How many eyes does a school have?*

Though both my parents worked, there was not a lot of money for extras, like pretty clothes, or accessories; little things that weren't really necessary but vital to a teen-ager. So when one of my teachers, who lived nearby, asked me to babysit, I jumped at the chance. I could finally buy those pretty red Capezzio shoes! But they were expensive, almost nine dollars. Now I could save up for them. At fifty cents an hour, it might take awhile, but I was happy to wait. Mr. Phillips knew me and still trusted me with his kids. I was determined to be a good sitter.

"Would it be all right if you went home by yourself tonight?" Mr. Phillips asked. "I'm kind of tired."

"Sure, it's only a block away," I replied. I was well on my way when I heard footsteps behind me. I quickened my gait, with only a swift glance at the shadowy figure at my back; to my horror so did the shadow. With just a few yards to get to my back door, I began to run... he did, too.

Made it! I was breathless when I slammed the door and locked it. We never locked doors in those days, so eyebrows were raised when I turned the key. My mother and her card playing cronies were all in the kitchen. I just ran upstairs to my room, breathless, and frightened. No one asked.

No one asked at another time, either...

Miss Charles, who lived across the street on Hunterdon, taught me to play the piano. Since we had no piano and my grandmother did, after school on Friday I would take two buses, walk through Belleville Park and cross a highway to my grandma's house. There I would practice over the weekend, and go home on Sunday night. I was only eight years old at the time.

One weekend walking through the park I could smell the fall. As I shuffled through the leaves, head down, admiring the orange and red colors, I heard someone coming up behind me. Turning slightly, I saw a man in sweats walking swiftly towards me. I picked up my pace. He did too. I began to run. He reached for me. By now I was out of breath; I couldn't even scream! My heart was thumping so loudly in my chest. I thought I could hear it! The blood was pounding in my ears. God, was I going to die? A couple turned onto the path. They realized immediately what was happening and yelled out, "Let that child alone!" The man ran past me and kept on going. Bless those people, whoever they were. They walked me the rest of the way and saw me safely to my grandmother's. She never asked me who they were.

I was never afraid until the park attack, and still I had to make that trip again, the next week.

All the fears I grew up with were a part of me now, and controlled my vision of the world. I still shudder at the sound of a siren, and when the electricity goes off and I'm in total darkness. My brothers aren't around to watch over me anymore. As a child I had no fear of bullies or bogeymen. My fears were of the war; air raids, dark green shades that were pulled down when the sirens sounded. I was afraid, too, when my mom came home with burn holes in her clothes. Her job in the factory was making plane parts and ammunition, and despite the lead apron she wore while riveting, sparks would burn her clothing. I didn't realize until many years later that I should have been proud of my mother at the time. *Too little, too late.*

As I turned off Hunterdon Street onto Hawthorne Avenue, headed for the Parkway, I passed the park that I had loved and feared. I opened the window, took a deep breath of fresh air, and aimed the car towards home.

I finally fit into the life style of 'clamdiggers'; people born to the sand and the sea. For the longest time I felt misplaced, still thinking of the city as my true home. Folks here still notice my city accent, though I've been here it seems, forever. I now consider myself a transplanted city brat, who finally got Tony Santos to realize that he loved me!

20

# *A Girl Dog*

Space was at a premium, in our home. Each of us carving out room for our daily dance. That numb, tap, tap, tap, that says you're alive – but not really. My dance was the same each day, a sojourn through chores that reminded me; I was a daughter in a field of sons.

The order of life perplexed me; why I seemed to offer no value, yet I was the one with all the skills. The one who could make a home where there was none. I could feed and clothe, though I bore no offspring of my own. But there was an order to things and perplexed or not, I lived with it. Andrew did not cook or clean, Kevin didn't sew. Raymond worked after school, so he was excused from all consideration. And Vincent, the oldest was a Vietnam Veteran, home in one piece. I should not only be grateful to have him back, it should be my privilege to clean and scrub around him.

My mother struggled to find her own space. It wasn't at her key punch operator job or the short stint she did as middle school librarian. "Too many women buzzing around," she said. And women simply didn't make good friends. "They were too busy trying to cut you down. They were always threatened by a smarter or more assertive woman." That's why all Mom's good friends were men.

Most days – good days, I was invisible. An unseen phantom who ordered their chaotic world. But sometimes there wasn't enough fog to cloud my presence. The days when even Johnny Walker could not put enough mist in the air to hide me. Those days, Mom would tell me of her despair raising a girl. How she'd spent a lifetime praying that God would never give her a girl; only to rescind that prayer years later because she was lonely in her world of men.

"Girls are much harder to raise," she said. "They were difficult. They wore their skirts too short and their jeans too tight and caught the eyes of the live-in-lovers. They were weak-minded and undisciplined. You could spend a lifetime watching them like a hawk and then one day without warning, they would rebel, talk back, stand up straight or think out loud. They would run away for love but regret it in the end."

I remember once, Mommy's *spirits* had actually led her to a tender moment. A rare Friday night when the mere sight of me didn't enrage her. She told me that her harshness was actually to protect me. The world was cruel and far too tempting for young girls. "They'll tell you – you can have everything and then grant you nothing. And eventually, you'll settle for what you can get. And what you get, is nothing good." Then she held me by the shoulders and said, "If I'm not vigilant, you'll end up just like me, with nothing good; cause inside you, is nothing good. Inside all women, is nothing good."

My father had long since left. It took years to hear the bits and pieces of the "reasons why," though our daily lives told enough of the story. We navigated through fights and arguments, avoiding neighbors when things spilled outdoors. My father said he could never make her happy. "She's a miserable and bitter woman," he used to say. And to most people, my mother did seem bitter. Her joy was usually invisible. But I could see it. I could touch it. I could measure it, count it, tell you how wide and deep it was any day of the week – because it reflected itself onto me. On joyful days, she'd tell me wondrous stories of her life in Detroit. How she and her favorite cousin, Tee, spent their days working together in the old Ford Plant, planning their futures. She'd talk about her dreams of being a fashion model, a business woman or even an accountant. She would seem wistful and pensive.

But on bitter days, I would discover the secrets of her heart; her abandoned life – waiting for Aunt Annie to rescue her. A smooth talking married man who stole her life away. A house full of children whose mere existence robbed her youth. And I was the symbol of what she'd lost. Bitter days were like survival days, when simply waking up in the morning was a challenge to her authority. And I measured my life in survival days. Getting through each one was like aging a whole year. In the world's eyes I was only 12, but in survival days, I was 18 years old.

I was ecstatic when another girl joined the family. Trinka came as a gift from our neighbor, Mr. Lundy. His dog had given birth to eight; seven male and one female. There was an all black male, who barked incessantly. He seemed aggressive and tough. Mom wanted him really bad! But Mr. Lundy was looking for a deal; "*take the girl dog off my hands and you can have that boy for free.*" Mommy wasn't at all interested in a female dog; she said they were scared and un-trainable. But since they were free, Mommy took the deal. Chince and Trinka came home with us that day.

My daily chores increased. Andrew and Kevin left for school far too early to walk and feed the dogs. And though my school started just twenty minutes after theirs', *surely there was enough time for me to fit this in.* I simply got up earlier.

Chince was a beautiful dog, even I had to admit that. His ears were constantly pointed upward. His neck was thick and strong, his coat, luxurious and shiny. It was indeed a pleasure to experience the praises and compliments, when I walked him. "*He's so gorgeous and strong. His coat is so shiny. Is he pure breed?*" I felt like my mother with her pride in her sons.

Trinka liked to walk without a leash. She didn't need one. Her steps would always mirror mine. Whenever she needed to stop, she'd simply nudge my leg to get my attention. She was with me constantly; when I laughed, when I cried, when I sat alone in my room wishing I could fly away, she was with me. It seemed she could feel my emotions, before I did. But she wasn't at all what my mother said. Trinka feared nothing. She was just as aggressive and protective as Chince. She just didn't bark. The incessant announcement of strangers and smells and rodent animals didn't interest her. Her joy was in the defense.

One night, we sat on the front porch with the interior lights down low. We kept the screen door open, hoping to get a breeze. From the street, I'm sure strangers thought it was an unguarded house with the front door left open. Kevin and Vincent were sitting on one side, my mother and I on the other. Trinka sat right in the doorway crouched down low. Her dark hair made her unseen. A man started walking up our pathway. My mother whispered, "do any of you know this guy?"

He kept walking towards the house, stretching his neck to see inside. Trinka sat still; no movement, no sound. She let the man reach the first step and without warning, she leaped. She took the entire stoop in one jump, landed on his chest, her mouth at his throat. Chince finally came to join her.

We later discovered that the man was certainly looking for a home to rob. He'd done it several times before. One officer implied that we were *supposed* to have a 'Beware of Dog' sign in the front yard. The other officer simply gave Vincent a high-five and Trinka a good pat.

I was surprised when Mommy acknowledged Trinka's prowess that day. She was proud of her, though she attributed Trinka's methods to the *cunningness* of being female. "That's cause she's a girl dog," Mom said. "She's like a sneaky woman. She let the man come to the steps and think it's safe and then attacked."

I was sure someday Trinka would make a great mother; she protected, she loved, she hunted. Moles and squirrels who dared enter our yard, usually found their fate at her hands. She chased and stalked them constantly. And sometimes, she'd catch them. Occasionally, I'd find her bounty presented to me at the back door; as if I was to clean and cook it for our meal. Luckily, my gratitude was enough.

\* \* \*

The day my mother feared came in early spring of 1972. The day I talked back, stood up straight and thought out loud. Johnny Walker and all his spirits visited our home the entire day. Mommy, Vincent and friends sat around commiserating on the world. For Vincent, it was a college education he'd been robbed of and a world unappreciative. His future was an uncertain mush his mind could not face. But for Mom, it was even deeper. She cursed her mother who had left her with relatives, so she could run off with her live-in man. She cursed my father because he'd found love in her sister; an affair never proven to be true. But to Mommy it didn't matter. It was further proof, that *'inside all women, was nothing good.'*

She yelled for me to come downstairs. As always, whenever they drank, I would retreat upstairs. There, I would carve out my peaceful space; doing my homework, writing, or being with Trinka. But inevitably, she would call me downstairs to turn the TV channel, bring her the phone or pour her another drink. This time, it was the latter; *'another Johnny and soda, very little ice.'* I had developed the skill of pouring more soda than Johnny. Whenever the days had waxed long, they could never tell what they were drinking. But this time, she wanted a good boost. Twice, she told me to increase the scotch. I tilted the bottle and shoved in the seltzer. Twice, I failed to meet her expectations.

The third time was my last. I didn't realize that she had followed me back into the kitchen. She saw my fake pour; letting the bottle tilt but nothing actually going into her glass. At first she just yelled, "you actually think you can out-smart me?" I was a bitch for even trying! She hit me across the face and snatched her glass from my hand. My face was on fire. She wanted an explanation. At first, I thought I should lie; it would be the easy way out. But then I simply told her the truth, "you've had enough. I thought you could save some for tomorrow."

Again she swung. She pushed my shoulder and I fell against the stove. I wasn't aware that I had screamed, but I could feel my own tears pouring along my open mouth. Trinka came quickly. She moved between me and my mother whining and whimpering, as if begging us not to force her to choose. Mommy yelled louder. She raised her arm simply to point her finger, but Trinka jumped! She snapped at Mommy and growled; backing up into me, but staying between us.

"Get that damn dog out of here!" She pointed her finger towards the back door but Trinka didn't move. She'd stopped growling but continued to whimper. I knew the commotion was confusing her. She

25

loved Mom and didn't want to bite her, but she had truly become "my" dog.

The others finally gathered in the kitchen. Mommy tried to make light of the whole thing. She told them, "oh please, that girl cries over everything. I didn't slap her all that hard! That's just drama so she can get some pity. You know Celia's game. She's just trying to turn you boys against me." Mommy left the kitchen grabbing the very same diluted drink I had fixed her.

Raymond sent me upstairs. He told me to grab some chicken and coleslaw and stay out of sight for a while. I was happy to get away. I snatched two of the cupcakes Andrew had brought home from Sweet Clover Dairy; one for me and one for the girl dog. We would sit and share my special day. After all, in survival days, I had just turned 19.

# *Lessons*

---·◆·---

# *Secrets*

Lisa was the first of her group to leave home. Her friends circled around her room like witnesses at a wake as she nervously stuffed her last minute possessions into any available bag…Humphrey Beargart, her Beatrice Potter books, the Renoir print, the icons of childhood and friendship. They formed a human chain like a wailing wall and then the car was packed, the tears spent and she and her mom, Patsy, were off.

Lisa's parents had acquiesced to this major leap for their little girl, a girl focused on studying Shakespeare where Shakespeare had lived and worked. It was the culmination of some difficult years, years when Patsy was sad and removed, Lisa fierce and determined to find her way. Yet she still felt the protective mother, ushering her child into adulthood.

The week had rushed by in a tangle of emotions, as Patsy and her daughter, Lisa, swept through London attending teas, meeting the faculty, moving Lisa in to her dorm room in Hyde Park where she was going to college for a year.

If you saw them together you may not notice the tension beneath the seemingly happy pair. Photographs reveal a blossoming eighteen year old with long tawny blond hair smiling next to a woman still youthful looking in jeans but with some streaks of gray in her brown hair. People often said they had the same smile, bright and open and quick to crack the façade lying dormant underneath.

They set off together in a jumble of books and luggage and settled into a small hotel on Oxford Street. It was a healing week, unusually warm in London late in the summer as they spent their days at Windsor Castle, The Tower of London or Westminster Abbey, taking the underground, finding their way. In the evenings they would curl up together in the big bed in the small crowded room and talk and munch on snacks, laughing at British television.

They found their way to the college on the opposite side of Hyde Park on a street of neatly fashioned brownstones with elegant doors and wide bay windows open to the trees and flowers. There it was, a simple brass plaque announced itself, "Ithaca College London."

The day of her move to the dorm seemed to come quickly as they piled the crammed suitcases into a cab. One by one, bright, expectant, smart faces climbed the narrow stairs to the dorm rooms tucked away over a Chinese restaurant and Lisa met her roommate, a girl from the Bahamas. Posters went up, books were unpacked, clothes piled high on the beds. They did a last minute checklist for towels and underwear and warm sweaters. And then it was done. Time to say goodbye. They walked to the Gloucester Street underground. Patsy turned to watch Lisa as she passed the pub, the launderette, the chemists and a Vietnamese restaurant, then turned into the entrance to her dorm, a walk up above the restaurant, perhaps a room with a view. She didn't look back.

All alone, all alone in London for the next twenty four hours, Patsy felt that pull, that exhilaration of invisibility, the invisibility she could not sustain in a world of too many people with too much to say.

The doorman welcomed her as she walked into the bar. It was 12:00 noon on a bright fall day in London. "I'll have a vodka martini, please." No one will ever know.

# *The Day I Left*

She didn't even bother to get up. She just laid there, motionless, staring intently at the colorless screen, absorbing the daily lives of characters far too plastic to survive in our rigid world. Her gray rooted strands wisped wildly across her face. The crumpled bed, filled with newspapers and circulars, reflected the disarray of our lives. It left her lost and unfeeling, sorting through a world of black and white.

My words seemed to fade into the air. There were no echoes when I repeated my announcement, "I'll be leaving in five minutes." I took a step back and motioned towards the door, thinking the threat of finality would move her to speak. But she said nothing.

I wanted to say goodbye. I wanted to tell her that despite her sheltered heart, I would miss her voice. Her numbness had become my sense of stability; the way the world seemed right. I needed her words, whether harsh or warm; just something to say letting go was OK. And I would let go, there would be no turning back. I was leaving. At 16, I would move 400 miles away. I would sleep away from her care, for the first time in my life.

My world had become increasingly smaller these last two years. Privileges were few and far between. Her suspicions had driven her to a place where all girls my age were wanton, promiscuous, obligated to their temptations. In her mind, I wanted everything that was wrong;

capable of nothing that was right. I had stopped asking to go to dances or parties. Even parental supervision and a brightly lit location wasn't enough to convince her there was no deception.

My friends no longer believed my stories. The lies I told of why I couldn't attend the band trip, the 10th grade dance or the science fair outing had become redundant. That dear aunt of mine had been sick far too many times. Why I didn't simply tell them the truth I don't know; that my mother was strict and that I wasn't allowed to date or go to parties. I suppose my lack of normal trust and privileges embarrassed me.

At 16, I knew a senior year of this would be worse. There would be parties and teacher chaperoned weekends, none of which I'd be able to attend. Like always, she would suggest that such outings were just a ruse young girls like me used to sneak away and meet men. When I turned 15, I almost thought she'd changed her mind about me. I asked if I could go on a ski trip, especially if I raised all the money myself. She said yes and I thought I was on my way. I raised the entire fee and even more. In fact, I was second only to Leslie Marks. But then suddenly, she changed her mind. She said, "chaperones or not, you don't need to be hanging out with all those *fast* girls. I know what's in your head and I'm not letting it happen."

I learned about the University's early admit program from a flyer outside my advisor's office. A shiny, laminated brochure pinned to her corkboard. Burnt orange, gold and rustic red leaves dotted the landscape around stone and mortar buildings. Students walked with backpacks and rode bikes. Others were scattered on sprawling lawns, reading and tossing Frisbees. I wanted to live inside that color brochure.

My advisor said I met the qualifications, but that early admit selection was competitive. I had to attend their four week program just to be considered. Only then and if I did well, could I be amongst the handful of students offered the scholarships. "You'll be competing against other 11th graders," she told me, "all with the same intentions. You might not be selected."

"None of that matters," I told her. "One of those scholarships will be mine."

I convinced my mother to let me go, by merely lying; something I was normally petrified to do. I told her that the scholarship was *already* mine, all I had to do is attend the summer program. I kept the story short, hoping all she would care about was the scholarship.

Two days before I was supposed to leave, she and Kevin got in
a fight. A bad one. She ended up throwing both he and Andrew out of
the house; leaving me alone with her. It was the same old fight they'd
been having for years. Kevin was smoking marijuana in her house. Even
though Andrew hadn't done it, he got included on "General Purpose." I
narrowly escaped because I pretended to have a cold; way too sick to have
anything to do with their ill behavior. Though I had never smoked, she
liked to say I was their lookout.

It took me just one day to pack. There wasn't much, just my
clothes and an old typewriter. I asked my mother if I could take the
small lamp in my room but she didn't answer. She spent the whole day
lying in her bed, reading the newspaper and watching TV.

I kept thinking, maybe she doesn't know that this is it; that I
would no longer walk through the door and assume her role. I kept
wondering, when would it be like it was when Andrew left? When
would they form a line in the driveway and wish me well, as though I was
an officer departing the ship? When Andrew left for college, we stood
in a line hugging and crying, bidding him farewell. And Mommy was
there in the front, weeping, squeezing, giving out her last minute advice;
those final words to summarize a lifetime of teaching, hoping she hadn't
missed something along the way. But for me, there was silence, a numb
heartbeat that I was to take as my only farewell.

Kevin had promised to drive me to the bus terminal, but I faced
facts after missing the 6 and 8 pm departures. My farewell line was
empty.

I quietly called her name again, hoping to get her attention. I
said goodbye and reminded her that I would call once I arrived. "It
will be early in the morning," I whispered. "I'll call before I head to the
registrars' office. Classes start tomorrow."

In a faint movement, she seemed to nod her head, but her eyes
remained locked on the screen. She leaned forward and turned the
channel. A commercial made her giggle.

I lifted my remaining shoulder bag, certain that I'd heard my cab
beep out front. She never turned her head.

"Close my door on your way out," she finally spoke.

"Sure." I left quietly, peacefully, accepting the numbness I'd come
to know as home.

# *Author*

you want to know why I write?
it's easier than
prayer.
cause I heard,
God's not talking to me.

I must've pissed Him off
that day last year,
when I asked Him to kill my employer.

I know it was wrong,
it's just that gut reaction,
when someone's pounding your head!

boss kept
jigging and jabbing,
cutting my psyche,
in ways God didn't mean.

and he thinks I don't know
about the game he's been playing –
telling the others to leave me out.

that's why I asked God
to *nix* his behind –
I just couldn't take it anymore.

then, my Mother,
she died,
after living a life,
of wishing
and pissing on graves.

that's when I knew
I'd better get straight.
else I'd die like her:
broke,

alone –
still waiting
for my number to hit.

This year I asked Him
to save my friend –
his body parts had
gone expired.

we tried begging
and borrowing
some leftover parts
but none of them would make him live.

So I quit praying,
or even
speaking to God.
It was sort of a mutual decision.
I agreed to write my heart and
He agreed to save it.

## *Bleeding Hearts*

The die cut hearts and cupids spilled out of the plastic bag liked plump confetti. Paper doilies, red silk ribbon and markers, Elmer's glue, scissors and a long, long list of names covered a corner of the table. Lisa pushed her blonde bangs away from her eyes eager to get started. "Mom, mom, can we do them now?"

My son, J.R., shrugged by to open the fridge, stood there staring into it. Did you ever notice how kids open a fridge and just stand there, looking or waiting for food to metamorphasize into their hand? "Yuck," he said, "Valentine's Day. Stupid."

He grabbed a Popsicle out of the freezer, wagged it front of his sister's face, "Who do you love, who do you love?" he teased. "MOM!" she yelled. Since J.R. was now in middle school his demeanor had developed a pre pubescent swagger the same day his voice changed.

Once again I was the class mother, head of the telephone tree for snow days, coordinator of every frickin' holiday party in the fourth grade. I did it for J.R., now once again I was in the pit of elementary school hell. Three dozen cupcakes were in the oven, still to be frosted in pink and white cream and topped with a little heart candy that might say "I love you", or "You are my sweet," or whatever. Cupcakes were not my thing. They either burned on the bottom, sagged in the middle, or stuck to the pan. Usually by the time they were transported to school they were lopsided and unattractive and there was usually some bratty kid who said, "My mother makes nicer cupcakes."

Fuck them.

"I want to make a special heart for Jamie, and one for Sherry and one for Jackie." Lisa started rummaging through the supplies. "Mom, I can't find my scissors." She was left-handed and required special scissors that vanished like socks in the dryer whenever she needed them. "Honey, when was the last time you had them." Her lip trembled, "I don't know." "Well, I'll help you cut with my scissors." "No, no. I want to do it. I want to do it."

I took a sip of scotch from the shelf on the kitchen divider just in time for the oven bell. "Not now, Lisa, I have to get the cupcakes out of the oven. Start filling out the cards you want to send." "Mom, everybody gets a card." Well, of course. This was the world of no child left behind, no hard feelings, no counting who's the most popular, no slap in the ego, no life lessons learned. We are all equal. Sure, beauty, brains and a degree from Harvard mean nothing. We are all equal.

Who thinks up these Hallmark holidays anyway? Maybe the Jehovah's have the right idea. They celebrate nothing. Just the other day Jenny came to my door with a Lighthouse pamphlet. Of course I had to let her in. Her son went to school with J.R., even received First Holy Communion together. Then for reasons beyond anyone's comprehension Jenny joined the Jehovah's, so now she traipsed the neighborhood ringing doorbells. Michael was no longer allowed to participate in parties, sports, or celebrations of any kind. Jenny sure wasn't home baking cupcakes. I suppose it is better then bearing the tears of your child who didn't get a card from Timmy.

I opened the jar of creamy pink frosting, found a spatula and began smoothing it on the crooked cupcakes. Lisa had temporarily given up on the scissors and was neatly writing names on little square white envelopes.

When I was little and had a schoolgirl crush on Edward Frick, he with his smooth shiny hair and nice skin, not everyone got a Valentine. The popular kids came home with brimming bags of love, and the losers ran home to Mommy, empty handed, crying, "Nobody loves me." These were the kids who won MacArthur Fellowships and ran

Exxon. After school the kids counted their lovers, oohing and aahing at raggedy doilies and glued on hearts. There were also secret Valentines, which made anything possible, especially giggles and secrets of ten-year-old unrequited love. Ah, love. I was shy with boys and didn't have the sangfroid so many little girls seem to understand intuitively. Then one Valentine's day there it was, a card from Edward Frick!!! My heart pounded so hard so couldn't look at him for a week.

I had the special heart boxes all wrapped and ready for the kids tomorrow, and a big box of Russell Stover for Tom. He enjoyed candy, but the card for Tom was always a problem. Our marriage was like a purgatory, brimming with the hot ashes of anger and disillusionment, on the cusp of descent or elevation. He drank his way through fifty states and how many countries with the high living media people at his job in television news. I was alone. Alone when he was away on long assignments. Alone when he was home. I was tired. I was angry. And now he was sober, but I couldn't clap my hands to "light on" and bathe in its glow. I was fermenting like raisins in a pot of gin.

His hell had been my hell too. "My dearest true love, my heart is filled with thoughts of you. Each day I am blessed by your presence and your love. I thank God for the day I found you." Sure. Who writes this shit anyway?

I was burying deep into my corner of remorse. He would come home tomorrow from his trip with candy and a card and I would smile and say, "Thank you, dear," and the elephant on the kitchen table would wink, but not move. It was all too heavy.

I sat down to help Lisa stack up her cards and compliment her on her handwriting. We put the hearts on the frosting and the cupcakes on platters. They were passable, a pink and white mirage of make believe happiness.

Tomorrow I'd pack them carefully in the car along with a couple of gallons of juice, put on my class mother smile and bring them to Mrs. O'Brien. I'd grin and pour, grin and pour, and help hand out the Valentines. I'd feel inept but wouldn't show it.

The things I was good at didn't count in this cut off world of casseroles and jelly molds like the one green bubbly thing I made that collapsed. I was ensconced in suburban fantasy in a town without sidewalks, perched on a ridge of the Ramapo Mountains, nestled in a world of chance, so alien from my New York streets, so alien from the razzle dazzle, the job I loved, the professional kudos, the Rob Roy's at lunch, little black dresses and jazz joints. And yet, Ringwood had a cockeyed charm. Surrounded by mountains and lakes, houses perched atop steep driveways, or no driveways at all. Some nestled so close to the lake one can only see a hint of a window and the eave of a roof. Log cabins rumble close to A-frames and A-frames tilt towards split-levels or Capes. All streets meander as they roll one into the other, frolicking upward and downward, even spiraling. Bordered by two magnificent and historic State Parks, there are miles of tranquil beauty the residents felt was their backyard. The main artery is called Skyline Drive, a serpentine two-lane road that connects Ringwood to the lower counties on their way to the George Washington Bridge. Forty-five minutes from Broadway, so close yet so far away.

Sometimes my brain felt entangled like a Cirque de Soleil without a net. I knew I thought too much, ruminated over foolish moments in time better left alone. The inner self I so steadfastly tried to nurture was splitting like an atom bombarded by "the others." I was a fraud, a puppet whose smile covered the grimace within as I went to teas and luncheons with perfectly set Limoge. My mind always racing, and then my heart when a major anxiety attack slammed me down.

But for now the tremulous and troubled cupcakes beckoned, and I took two for the kids before they went to sleep. Lisa was getting tired, her eagerness fading and the left handed scissors forgotten for now. We cleaned up the ribbons and doilies and markers, and put the cards in a shoebox. I had to think about dinner for tomorrow night for after all, it was Valentine's Day and Tom would be home.

# Roots

## *Boomer Fatigue*

I am of a generation without a name, sandwiched in the glitch of history, a blip on the demographic charts. After the Victorian Era the Twentieth Century blasted into consciousness with the Golden Age, soon followed by the Jazz Generation, the Lost Generation, The Great Generation, The Baby Boomers, The Me Generation, Generation X , Generation Y and now something called the Millenium's. Like someone with a dysfunctional astrological chart, my cohorts and I were born on the lower cusp of the ubiquitous Baby Boomers, and most of us were either married and raising children or working as white gloved secretaries when the soft spoken, folk singing, rhythm and blues sixties turned radical and the Sexual Revolution was born.

It was the first roar of the "Baby" giant, and although I was older by a few years the wake of their tidal wave kept sucking me into the world according to Boomers as they kept coming and coming and coming. And like the old Irish folk tune, "They Were All Out of Step but Jim" I found the fissure of floundering in history disconcerting and a bit frightening. What ever happened to hanging out with the guys, slinging back a few gin and tonics, waiting for the phone to ring? The fresh air fun and beer parties in the Hamptons and the Wednesday night meet ups in the city turned into a fearsome battle with snarky guys looking for a one-night stand. Just like there were "good girls" who came of age in the late fifties, so too there were "good guys" who fooled around but were not by any means experienced sexual studs, guys who knew girls like us didn't put out, guys who were protective, not predatory.

I felt I was extinct as my little black dress, a dinosaur of a kinder, gentler time. I was twenty-seven and single in 1965, working at ABC News, going to college at night, trying to break the glass ceiling before the term existed. Now the rules had changed and I felt stranded in a time warp, just out there, isolated in a mindset left in the dust by sex, drugs and rock and roll. It was a lonely time.

The tragedy of Vietnam knocked on my door in 1968 when my cousin, Eugene O'Connell was killed in action in Vietnam. Handsome, talented, and an only child he was only twenty-two years of age. A month later Martin Luther King was assassiniated, then Robert Kennedy. The tumult was palpable, but I had only been an observer, not a participant in the generational chasm.

When the Women's Liberation Movement opened the doors to other ways of being, I approached cautiously. I was now ensconced with two little kids in the suburbs, wondering how the hell I got there. That first wave of feminism was strident, angry, forceful, and powerful. Marriages were on the skids as women left their husbands to find themselves. I used the movement to finish college. Since I was a returning woman, as they said, all I had to do was sign up. The course was called Women in a Contemporary Society. The rhetoric was radical, but I was in college, being nurtured, being guided. It was a powerful time. I got my degree with honors. Was I becoming an older, make believe Boomer?

I may have gained some momentum, but I still didn't measure up. The Consciousness Raising group I joined chastised me for my ineptitude in sharing. Evidently my conscience was not up to par. I was raised after all to be a good girl, wife, mother, not a woman who spoke of herself like she really mattered.

I once heard in a Sociology class that the Boomers are like a giant pig eaten by a snake that changes everything about the snake as it moves through it. How apt. For forty years their wants, needs, and desires have influenced the fashions I wear, the movies I see, the books I read, and the television shows I may or may not watch. Why would I care about those whiny Thirty-Something's?   Now the little darlings are going gray and the retirement lobby and the Social Security Administration quake at their next demand. Will they retire early? Will they drain the entitlement funds? The real estate section of the paper is awash with the constant barrage of luxury retirement communities.

Ha, does the no-name generation ever get credit for Elvis, Chubby Checker and the Platters? Does the no-name generation ever get credit for I Love Lucy and The Honeymooners? Does the no-name generation ever get credit for fidelity and long lasting marriages and Valium? I don't think so.

When my Newsweek arrives on Monday morning I cringe when it's another Boomer File issue. Frankly, I don't give a damn. They still exist. They changed the world. Enough, I say. I'm tired of them. I did, however, get my full Social Security benefits at age sixty-five, just under the wire for the new requirement age of sixty-seven.  I guess sometimes it pays to be irrelevant.

꧁✿꧂

# *Mary*

No one paid attention to the rooster that kept goose-stepping nervously back and forth, in staccato fashion, across the three-cushioned couch taking up one whole wall of the kitchen. Mary's eccentricity was well known. No one even questioned her choice of a house pet. A rooster was always present in the room. We children were afraid of him, but the grown-ups would just shoo him away if he got obnoxious. One strange thing about the brown feathered bird; you never saw traces of him in the house. The red flowered bulk of the sofa that the rooster commandeered matched nothing in the room, thus making it obvious that Mary was 'sense of style' challenged. This didn't bother her, nor did it bother the others. We were all used to her haphazard décor. This place was not a showplace; it was a house that welcomed you.

Voices were raised up and over other voices, a cacophony of sounds becoming one buzzing roar. English, Italian, and Portuguese could be heard, but not understood by any one person, for they were all speaking at once. People were trying to listen to each other, but hearing no one voice clearly. It was a meeting of friendly chaos.

I watched as she puffed on her Chesterfield and looked around the room. The place was crowded with people, all there to celebrate Mary's 90th birthday. Her kitchen was full of family; sons and daughters, cousins, and grandchildren, including me. Friends and neighbors, too, were all contained within its creamy yellow walls. As kitchens go, it had the usual table and chairs; wooden, worn, and scratched, but clean. Clean, yes, but neat-not always. Sheer white curtains hung carelessly from plain metal rods. The room was thick with people and good cheer. The guest of honor might well have been invisible, I thought, for folks who hadn't seen each other in ages were getting reacquainted, and for the moment anyway, they were ignoring my grandmother. Mary didn't seem to mind, however. She wasn't used to all this fuss. She was just as content to smoke and reminisce. Soon enough the attention would turn to her and the business of being polite and enduring kisses and hugs from one and all would begin. No one seemed to realize that my grandma's stamina was not what it used to be. I could almost hear her thoughts- "I'm old, you peoples, leave me in peace!" But she knew that each and every friend and relative in her cozy kitchen was there out of love and respect for her.

I loved the kitchen's old coal stove with its black cast-iron kettles and pots boiling on it, the smell of sauce and meat wafting through the whole house. The apple and orange peels that were always on the stove tried, but failed, to overcome the scent of food. Normally they lent a delicious aroma to the room. Cigarette and cigar smoke made a haze over everyone's head. It hung like a spider web near the once white ceiling, dimming the light that hung loosely in the middle of the room. A kitchen window was open just enough to let stale smoke out and let some fresh air in. It wasn't working well, but no one complained; it was 1941 and smoking was still fashionable. Mary herself smoked from the time she was thirteen years old, she told me. Grandma never warned me of the hazards of tobacco; to her it was a natural thing to do.

"I bin in this country 82 years," she whispered to me. I sat close to her, glad that she was confiding in me. Memories flooded back to her. "I can still remember how hoppy and scared, too, I felt when my mama sent for me."

Mary's mother, Rose Rinaldi, left her husband and daughter in Italy and sailed to America, sometime in the 1850's. Why, Mary never knew. Rose just up and left their olive orchards and broke all family ties when she did so. Growing up, no one ever mentioned Rose's name, and Mary was too young to form the questions needed to learn about the mother who abandoned her.

Not until Mary was eight years old did Rose send for her only child. At eight, my grandmother was old enough to work and make money for her mother, who would bring the child to the factory and teach her the intricacies of sewing dolls' clothes. In those days, the 1860's, if a child could sew, the parent got more money; no one need know the circumstances concerning child labor. Thankfully for all involved, Mary was healthy; a short, stocky sturdy little girl with a head of curly, reddish-brown hair. Young Mary had a haughty air about her which she never lost, possibly because she was taught by nuns in Italy to be a lady. There was an aura about Mary Rinaldi that almost demanded respect. Certainly we children were a little afraid of Grandma. Her appearance seemed very stern, but her softer side would show at times with a little pat on the head or a "Bella, Bella." (pretty, pretty)

Mom said that her grandfather was a judge in the Province of Catanzare, in Calabria, Italy, and had little or no time for his daughter. Mary was of no use to him in the orchards, and he was busy with politics. Joseph was not a 'hands–on' father. His workers received more attention from him than the child ever did. He didn't argue when his wife sent for their daughter to come to America. Little did he know or care what the girl might encounter in the new country. Mary herself must have had no idea what incredible joys *or* sorrows lay in store for her.

Grandma looked at me sitting there by her, and with a gentle pat on my head said, " Little gell, (girl) I remember when my mama met me at the dock. I din' know her; how can I rekanize her? Mama foun' me though." Listening to her, I could just imagine a lone child in a mass of adults, shaking with fear and excitement, a bandana on her head trying to contain that unruly curly hair. "Mama hugged me real tight; I was hoppy." It was one of the few hugs Mary would ever receive from her mother.

For a while Rose treated her like a little queen. Mary was content, even when her mother took her to the factory, and she was put to work. Soon enough, though, she learned what a taskmaster Rose was. At times she was physically abusive in spite of the child's efforts to do well and please her mother. In time, Mary became disillusioned with the new world and her mother's introduction to it. She was merely chattel to the woman. Still she did as she was told, for Mary was an obedient daughter.

Young Mary had little chance to rebel, however, for a mere few years later an older man came forward to ask for Mary's hand in marriage. The child was all of twelve and a half years old! Granted, she was pretty and her stocky body had become shapely, making her seem older than her age. She still had curly locks, and her face had thinned out some. Mary was also proud of her light skin, almost vain about it. Certain parts of Italy, usually the northern part, produced blondes, a far cry from the more common brunettes of the rest of the country. Though she wasn't from there, possibly an ancestor had migrated to Calabria, and Mary profited from the move, giving her a very fair skin. This was a desirable feature to have for some Italians.

Mary never dreamed her mother would give her away to this man with the mean brown eyes; but she did. Dominic Manglass was twenty- nine years old, a dark, olive-complexioned man of medium height. Mary was wedded and bedded in short shrift. Her life became a different hell from then on. For better or for worse, this was her lot in life and she accepted her fate with resignation once again. My mother sounded sad and sometimes angry when she spoke of my grandfather. I never thought of him in the familiar 'grandpa' way because of what she told me.

Dominic owned a bar in Newburgh, New York, and Rose lived in New Jersey, so Mary seldom saw her mother after the move. In the 1800's few people owned cars, so travel was limited. There was no lesser of two evils between her mother *or* her new husband. Both were unbearable. Mary was pregnant at thirteen-a baby having a baby. She wore the feed sacks that women 'with child' wore in those days. No maternity clothes then! Though large with child she had to climb the stairs in her new home many times a day. She'd trudge upstairs to cook for the customers, perhaps a huge pot of pastafagiole (macaroni with beans), then downstairs for the disgusting job of cleaning the spittoons that sat here and there throughout, on the old oak floors of the saloon. How she gagged the first few times she was forced to do this task and got a beating for it until she learned to control herself.

Grandma was being awfully quiet; I became worried. I touched her elbow. She shook her head a little and grumbled, "What you want?" She must have been daydreaming and I wanted badly to know what she was thinking. "Tell me, Grandma, what are you dreaming about?" And in her own broken English she exclaimed, "that somma-nu beach! I bored his children, I cleaned up after those pigs in the bar!" "Take it easy, Grandma, relax, it's all right." I said softly.

I knew the story of how she found out that Dominic was raising yet another family not far from their home. She got up enough nerve to leave him. It wasn't only that he cheated on her, but the fact was he had two daughters and two sons with the other woman and named them exactly the same as his first family! There was Asunta (Sue in Italian), Angela, Joseph and Dominic. Around the corner there was Asunta, Angela, Joseph and Dominic. The old goat took no chances that he would call his children by the wrong names.

Dominic had sent for a young woman from Italy. She spoke no English, and was not allowed to have friends outside the home. The deception was discovered because the children went to the same school. After talking to them, a teacher informed Mary of the strange coincidence. Mary went to the other woman and told her to keep Dominic, she didn't want him. She didn't make the children hate their father. The half-siblings became fast friends with hers, in spite of the gossip that flew throughout the neighborhood. They all stayed connected until Mary moved the family to New Jersey.

Here they were on Badger Avenue in Newark. Grandma told me how she made the children follow the railroad tracks nearby, to pick up pieces of coal that dropped off the train to feed the coal stove in the kitchen. The stove was the only source of heat in the house, and it was kept going all the time, except on hot summer days. Since boys were the hardest working, they were allowed to sleep behind the stove to keep warm. The girls slept in one of the cold bedrooms.

My grandmother was the first woman in her circle to wear slacks! It just wasn't done. Mary realized how comfortable they were when she donned a pair of overalls to dig out her cellar while constructing a wine-making area. I have a picture of her in those very overalls. Because she had developed a penchant for slacks she became known as Long Pants.

After her divorce, she was hard pressed to care for her four children, and since it was during Prohibition, she could make and sell her wine discreetly. People didn't know that on the side, Mary was bootlegging for the 'gang'. Nobody suspected that a mother with children in the car was delivering booze in the wheel walls of her car! Since she had become an independent young woman, she began to make money, which she invested by buying the homes around her. When she passed away, we found that Mary owned five houses on her block.

As she sat in the midst of the birthday revelers, a grin slid across her wrinkled cheeks, and I knew she was reminiscing again. I let her, though I would have loved to have heard about it. Grandma was short with children sometimes, and I didn't want her to tire of me.

Mary stirred-somebody was interrupting her thoughts. "Wha', what you want of me?" she complained. Looking around, she was bombarded by noise, voices, the smoky kitchen. It came back to her; she was in her own house, in the middle of her birthday party. The small crowded room had an air of good cheer, but I think Grandma wanted to stay in the past. She was getting tired of the fuss.

"Mom, they want to cut the cake." It was her daughter Sue. "C'mon, I'll help you." And so the party continued. Her children played Mary's favorite songs; "A Bicycle Built for Two," "Daisy, Daisy," and the "Tarantella," an old Italian dance. The kitchen table was pushed against a wall. The music pepped Mary up some, and she even danced a little, to everyone's delight. When she got out of breath they urged her to sit and rest.

"Good," she whispered to me. "They leave me 'lone now." She murmured something to herself, and closed her tired old lids. But too soon she was brought back once more to the present.

Now here she sat, not in her favorite pants, but in an old black cotton dress. She looked down at herself in distaste at the white collar, now yellowed with age that broke the starkness of the black. Mary grumbled to herself, "I no care. No new clothes at my age." She adjusted the dress and settled her bony body back in the kitchen chair. Her once strong hands were gnarled and arthritic from working so many years. The lines that decorated her face were her medals of honor; each one earned with care and worry and hard work. Her once warm dark eyes, now clouded with cataracts, closed briefly. Then Mary straightened up and stretched her old black cardigan tightly around her frail body. These days she felt cold even in warm weather. She shivered visibly.

"Mom, are you all right?" her daughter Sue asked. She had caught the trembling matriarch's discomfort.

"Of course Asunta, I'm hokay." After 82 years in this country, Mary never lost her accent. And though they were born in the states, her children still spoke Italian in her house. "No today, though, too many Medikhans (Americans) here." She winked at me, and I smiled back. As she lit another cigarette, Grandma relaxed and looked around her crowded kitchen crammed with well-wishers. My eyes fastened on the world-weary face. "How many more birthdays," she wondered tiredly. "How many more must I bear?"

Four more, though my grandma didn't know it at the time.

# *Thorpe Street*

I'd never seen her cry like that; a deep, hollow weeping that wails out slowly because all your insides are gone. She moved through the room, lost and frantic, searching for a closed-in space to hide the darkness of her heart. That she could love someone so deeply came as a surprise to me. I'd never seen my mother love. Her care for me had always been structured, regimented, as though she'd been receiving an hourly wage to raise me. A small, stout woman, who had long lost her doll-like figure. Her hair, still thick and wavy, maintained it's natural sandy hue. Her 40 years undetectable, hinted only by her weight. Home beckoned her; a native of Detroit and a small community called Thorpe Street.

\* \* \*

Uncle Tee died on Tuesday. I was chosen to accompany my mother to the funeral. On Thursday, I was pulled out of school and told we had scraped together enough money for two tickets to Detroit – just one way. The Detroit family would make sure we got back home. I was 9 and not quite sure what use I could be. Mourners needed soft things; their hands held, their shoulders squeezed tight. I could not remember a single time my mother's hand rested in mine or a moment of embrace. Her distance from me was the comfort I knew. I was sure one of my other siblings was better suited for this task.

My brother Andrew made it clear that this, my first plane ride, was not a pleasure trip. I was to mind her, keep quiet and not ask questions. I was to cause her no further pain than she had already suffered. But as I sat looking at the world from a height I'd never seen, it was difficult not to feel some joy and amazement.

The journey into sky was wondrous. Soft cotton clouds that seemed to dissipate in deference to our passing. The New York skyline bid us farewell, fading ever so quickly into tiny dots with flickering lights. I watched a single cloud grow closer and then fly along side us. On the ground, I used to look up and wonder about the people who passed through the sky. Were they free? Were their lives something to remember? Was their destination quiet and peaceful or bustling and exciting? I stared out the window and imagined myself alone on a journey to that far away place – the one all children dream of.

Andrew's instructions stayed with me and I sat quietly. My mother's numbness kept her in solitude. She sipped her lukewarm coffee, periodically doused with whiskey from her tiny silver flask. I wanted to ask, how Uncle Tee died and where would we stay in Detroit? But I kept quiet, waiting to glean the explanations from the things I overheard; just as I had always done.

When I was 7, I overheard my mother say that Tee was more like a big brother because he helped raise her, after her mother Ella re-married. They all lived in the house on Thorpe Street, but only Great-Aunt Annie's name was on the deed.

Mom always talked about Annie with such reverence and love, but the stories of her never seemed loving. When Grandma Ella fell in love with a dark skinned porter named George, Annie told Ella, she'd have to break up with him or leave the house. Annie used to say, "lighten up the family. Don't drag us into darkness." George was simply too black for Annie, his skin – like chocolate. Ella went off with George and left Mom and Uncle Nathan behind. Later, Annie sold Ella's share of the land they owned in Dearborn. How and why she did it, I never discovered.

Annie loved my mother's long sandy brown hair. Though Mommy was just as dark as her brother Nathan, her hair color made her appear lighter or of mixed ethnicity. Annie started a rumor that the family was part Chippewa Indian. It seemed to go well with Mom's long hair and Ella's broad nose. But years later, truth and a little research proved the family was nothing more than Nigerian immigrants and Georgian slaves.

Tee was dark. He had no special ethnic features, but he was kind and honest. He seemed to be the only one not mesmerized by my mother's hair. He kept her grounded, working hard to counteract Annie's influences. Tee and Mommy were close – spending most of their days together, working at the same factory. That was until the day she ran off to marry my father, Carl. He was a dark skinned seaman, working as a navy electrician – and much too dark for Annie. Annie refused her blessing on the marriage and insisted my mother give up her dark skinned beau. This seemed to be the thing that separated my mother from her Thorpe Street world and most likely, her tenderness.

We arrived in Detroit late afternoon. I had a hard time controlling my excitement over the landing; watching the flaps lower and the wind leave signature trails behind us; the city lights slowly coming into view; and the anticipation of the first wheels touching. I grinned slightly and coveted a knowing wink from the stewardess. She gave me golden colored wings with the airline's emblem. A souvenir I cherished for years.

Uncle Nathan picked us up in his latest Cadillac. Like most folks living in Detroit, he changed cars every year. I sat in the back, enjoying the temporary distance from my real world. I pretended traveling was my way of life – that this short journey to Michigan was actually Europe or Africa or the Far East. I imagined the slender necks of tall giraffes leaning to keep up with us; a street side market was off in the distance – people buying and selling red and golden fabrics. I saw the wonders of the world, right there on Interstate 94.

Eventually, I overheard more about Tee's death. I listened here and there, avoiding any long interruptions to my back seat fantasies. From what I gleaned, he died coming home from the bank. A cab driver took his $20 bill on a $5 fare. Tee tried yelling and demanding he come back. He never got a chance to chase the cab, the heart attack came quickly. Tee was 52.

One sixteen Thorpe Street was a three story Romanesque Victorian; stone and brick. The stone steps were high and the door was solid wood with beveled glass. It reminded me of New York brownstones, but it was set far back and had a large yard. Annie and Tee had lived there all their lives.

Our relatives owned most of the homes on Thorpe Street. Nathan lived across the street and two of his daughters on either side. Mom's cousins owned two other houses further down. The house next door to Annie was rented to a large family that looked Hawaiian, but maybe just mixed. They were introduced as relatives, but I suspected they were simply close friends with the right skin color for inclusion.

It took an hour before I ever saw Annie. She remained in her bedroom, too distraught to come out. Family members entered and exited her room, as though she was a Don, doling out approvals. I sat alone on the dark tufted couch playing with my wings and staring out the window. Once in a while, a new relative would come and introduce themselves, then marvel at how much I looked like my mother, only my skin and hair were darker.

I managed to get permission to move into the kitchen. There was food and soda. I heard Annie and Mommy talking in the hallway; their girlish-like whisper; sharing stories about Tee and his stubbornness. But they got quieter, whispering and hushing one another. Mommy told Annie that I was standing right in the kitchen so she shouldn't discuss such nonsense. As usual, it was something I was too young to hear, but I pretended to be looking for salt, leaning in the open cabinet so I could hear them better.

Annie took a hard breath. She sniffled back her tears. In a soft whisper, she confessed it had been a long time since she repeated the rumor. It was an evil story;  a lie – *that I was Uncle Tee's daughter*. A horrible story implying that Mommy and Tee's closeness was something more. I was shocked and disgusted. These foul words she dared repeat, despite the shame it implied. I knocked the salt down from the cabinet. It spilled across the counter.

Mommy hushed Annie lower, insisting it was a ridiculous thought, that I looked far too much like Carl to ever believe such a thing. I had his eyes, his nose and mannerisms. She was reminded of him, even when I spoke.

The rumor made me angry and ashamed, though I knew it wasn't true. There was so much of Carl in me and I was suddenly proud of any traits we shared. I resented Annie for saying this horrible thing. I resented being brought to Thorpe Street. I resented my mother for loving it so much.

Annie and Mommy emerged from the hallway. They gave one another a final hush. Then Mommy whispered, "Carl made me give up everything. Here I am, struggling in New York and he's running around town with every woman he can meet. If it wasn't for the kids and that house, I'd come back home. But I'll be damned, I ain't leaving – I'm keeping that house!"

Annie patted her back and consoled her with the knowledge that Tee always missed her. That his love for her was an ever protecting force. They entered the kitchen clutching their Kleenex and resuming their cry. With a casual greeting, Annie pinched my chin and said, I was a dark child, but looked mostly like my mother.

My first funeral was a lesson in hierarchy. Annie sat to the right, my mother next to her and Nathan, three or four people down. It seemed to be according to shade. I sat in the back with a distant cousin, charged with minding me. One by one, we passed in front of Annie, hugging her and acknowledging her grief.

My mother seemed genuinely broken by Tee's death. She cried throughout the weekend; sitting with her family; sharing their stories. With them, her voice was graceful, tender, almost child-like. An accent I'd never heard temporarily appeared. But the plane ride home was a return to solitude. She sipped her doused coffee and kept her eyes closed. Her only words to me were instructional; to pull my dress under me when I sat; to keep my feet on the floor; to be quiet when the stewardess was speaking. The distance I knew had returned.

\* \* \*

I only made two other visits to Thorpe Street. Once when Annie died and again, when Nathan died 10 years later. When my mother passed, I discovered that cousins had sold 116 Thorpe. Everyone had moved to the suburbs, which made sense to me. The family was now far too dark skinned to keep a home on Thorpe Street.

# Sandy's Place

before
the wind shoves me a corner gust,
before Mr. Armstead's dog races to the fence,
my intestines knot.

I hear the wave of speakeasy rhythms.

stopping to pick up a withered leaf,
my backpack falls, as I bend.

the porch light – red, as the stop,
flickers from pounding feet.
heavy women and quickened men.

pork soaked mustard greens,
turnips, tobacco and Tanqueray,
at a price you can afford.

one, last, deep breath –
then the maze of shined up soles.
I keep my eyes towards hell – but then,
he twists and turns,
a bump and grind –
I snatch my hand away and he stumbles.

"is that your daughter?" a woman screams.

but, he's too drunk to stand –
he just wiggles his pleasure up against her.

"got a body on her! – she does."

one lone pie pan, covered in foil
is still on the stove – my brothers
must've eaten and run.
age affords them the freedom to escape.

Mommy stops me
asks about my day,
then shows me off to Mrs. Lundy –

I'm wearing the same size bra as her.

just a short trip across the room, then
up the outside stairs.  I let Toby in from
the yard and give him half my plate. and

when the silence surrounds my plastered walls,
when my chest-of-drawers barricades the door,
I know I am safe.

## Give Us This Day

"Some day, when I'm a pro football player, I won't have to use a rig like this," Danny thought. He was setting up ropes across the attic alcove of the old garage in back of their house. This make-shift equipment was to prepare an exercise routine to tone up his body for football season. He made the ropes as taut as possible to form a sort of parallel bar from a set of beams that ran across the width of the garage. His plan was not to tell his parents about this. He knew they couldn't afford the equipment he needed to keep in shape, and if they knew, they would go broke trying to get it for him. A big strapping six footer, sixteen year old Danny Michaels slipped his ankle weights on, pondering his life as he busied himself.

"The father-son banquet is tonight, so I'd better not work out for too long. Besides, it's dad's birthday, too," he mused. "A boring evening for me, but it'll be nice for dad. He's so proud of me" Danny knew this with some modesty. Shy for the most part, he was extremely popular with both teachers and classmates.

"The girls are an extra bonus," he thought cheerfully. Being shy attracted the girls to him like bees to honey. He didn't have to adopt the 'macho' attitude that some of his buddies had. Danny's curly brown hair and green eyes helped with the teenage girls.

"I just wish there was more money to spend for dating, though."

He mulled over the disappointment that his parents wouldn't let him take a part-time job for fear that his grades might suffer. No cause for worry, really, because Danny was an honor student. He seemed to balance his busy athletic schedule and school subjects easily.

As he stood on a chair to reach the ropes, Danny thought about his mom. She worked hard, he knew. If only dad earned more money she wouldn't have to work at all. She would love to stay at home, making sure that he and his sister Dana were okay. Dana was a typical teenager, outgoing and hell bent to live life to the fullest. She was younger than him by two years, and was blessed with the same curly hair and green eyes; a very pretty girl she was, and popular with the boys. If Mom were home she'd slow down Dana's engine. He grinned to himself. Danny was mama's boy and he knew it. So did his sister. She was jealous of the fact that he and his mom could talk about anything and everything. Not so with his dad, though. Joe Michaels was quiet like Danny and two introverts don't make great conversation.

Standing on the chair, Danny grabbed one rope and with strong arms swung his legs up and over. His legs tangled around the other rope. Instinctively he wedged the back of his head under the far rope, trying to regain balance, but his body fell awkwardly. His throat caught between the now twisted ropes with such force that his neck snapped.

"My god, I can't breathe," he thought. "I'm strangling!" Danny struggled helplessly and in doing so knocked over the chair. Now he had lost his only hope of taking the weight off his noose-like position. Before he passed out, a prayer sprung to his lips…

OUR FATHER WHO ART IN HEAVEN…

"Dana! Have you seen Danny anywhere?" It was her dad, just coming home from work. "Am I my brother's keeper?" she thought sullenly. Aloud she answered, "No, dad, I haven't and I've been home for more than an hour. Aren't you two going to the father-son shindig tonight?"

"We're supposed to, but I'm not sure what time it is. Where's that kid , anyway? It's not like Danny to be this late coming home."

"'Course it isn't," Dana grumbled. "Mr. Goody Two Shoes; gets me in trouble 'cause I'm never in on time." Danny's thoughtfulness was always a thorn in her side. All she ever heard was, "why can't you get home right after school? Danny does. He doesn't worry us like you do. He's considerate." He's God, she thought ruefully.

HALLOWED BE THY NAME...

"I'll look around for him, dad, not to worry. First time he's late for anything and everybody panics," she grumbled. Dana walked outside and over to the garage. Her brother's bike was there, so he couldn't be far away. Looking about, she spotted one of his buddies passing by.

"Hey, Bill, seen Danny anywhere?"

"No, Day. After school he said he was heading home."

With that, Dana walked to the front porch and sat down gloomily. A neighbor waved to her. "Hey, kid, why so glum?"

"Looking for my brother. He seems to have gotten lost between school and home."

"Oh, he came home, all right. I saw him about three o'clock. Said he had a dinner date with his dad tonight."

Thoughtful now, Dana went inside. She heard the familiar sounds of the shower. Dad was more than a little anxious about this 'do' tonight, she could tell. Joe Michaels was basically a stay-at-home kind of guy, and didn't relish going out; especially to school functions.

The shower noises ceased and her dad yelled, "Is he back yet?"

"Nope!" she yelled back. As she walked to her bedroom, Dana looked in at Danny's room. "Mister Clean" she muttered. Another bone of contention. Her room looked like 'who did it and ran', while her brother's room was the epitome of neatness. Her folks let her know about that, too. Heaven and Hell they had nicknamed their rooms. Guess which was which.

THY KINGDOM COME...

By now Joe was worried. It was past five o'clock and still no Danny. He wished his wife, Lena, was home. She always knew what the kids' routines were and where they might be. "Working an early night shift was fouling up this whole family, he thought grumpily. I wish she'd stay home!"

"Selfish!" He reprimanded himself angrily. He was aware of the fact that Lena was doing what she had to do. Walking over and opening the back door, he hollered, "Dannneeeee!"

Inside the garage his father's voice floated up to Danny as he drifted in and out of painful consciousness. "Happy Birthday, Dad, was his last sad thought.

THY WILL BE DONE...

# Secrets

# Remnants

She remembers
the beige angora beret and scarf
   so rakishly appealing.
the soft cream turtle neck sweater
   so darling.
the simple pink strapless sundress
   so seductive
        puddling
            crinkled tissue
              to the floor.
The clothes she wore whenever they met.

She remembers
   the denim skirt,
       multicolored espadrilles,
          tan legs
His tallness, his darkness,
   blue Oxford shirt,
       sleeves rolled up
Bleaching her surroundings
   to anything
      but him.
The day she found him and lost herself.

She wanted
  the euphoria
She wanted
  the passion
She wanted this man who
  knew her in a world that never was.

Was there scotch on her breath
   as she soothed her
      crying daughter
Late again

Was there scotch on her breath
   as she slipped her way home
Filled
   with thoughts of him
   in a haze of mellow afternoons
Fumbling
   her brain
      cutting off
         her oxygen

Speaking
   lies
     to get her
       through the night.

Down and down
   she went
Deep into their
   fantasy
Fueled with
   self pity
Nourished by
   solitude
Drunk in
   the night.
Smiling a
   plastered smile
Betraying
   her family
Collateral damage

She remembers
   hollowed sunken eyes,
parchment lips.
 Fear

She remembers
    a narrow bed
        bilious green room
           a heavy steel door
Slammed
She remembers
    shuffling paper slippers
        gray sweats
Despair

No summer straw hat with
    grosgrain ribbon
        graces her head
No soft linen dress
    flows against her
        waiting skin.
Agony

All is done.

# *The Dance*

He deliberately thrust his pelvis against her, making her aware of his arousal. Heard the quick catch of breath. When he saw her lids go heavy, he knew the movement affected her. "Do you feel what you do to me?" he whispered in her ear.

They were on the dance floor in their favorite hangout; she, her husband, and their two friends. The guys were buddies from school and sports. The girls had known each other for ages. She wasn't on the floor with her husband. They often danced together, she and his friend, moving gracefully to the music; meshing, their rhythm in sync. But tonight their easy flow was lethal, an emotional danger zone.

"My god, are you crazy? Everyone can see what you're doing!" The words didn't ring true, however, for she leaned heavily against him, allowing him to pull her even closer to him. Her bones felt liquid, as if at any moment she would melt to the floor.

'Well, your hubby's already three sheets to the wind, and she's not far behind. Look at her, she's bumping and grinding all by herself. Let's go outside-nobody will miss us." The temptation was great. And she was weakening.

It was way after hours, and the owners locked up, leaving the customers in and everyone else out. This was a usual tactic, especially for a weekend. The place was dark and noisy. Smoke crept along the ceiling.

73

A mahogany bar, long and shiny, was full and three bodies deep. At ten minutes to two, people backed up their drinks, ordering two or three, as no one would be served after two o'clock. There was no fear of the police raiding the place; three officers were there already, drinking and dancing. This was a well known after hours bar for those in the know. The music at this hour ran to slow and bluesy, giving the room a sensual atmosphere.

She'd known that he was attracted to her for awhile now. She wasn't blind to the accidental touching and off-handed compliments. But up until now she wouldn't have dreamed of cheating on her guy. Tonight she was feeling the buzz of too much drink, and her dance partner's attention made her feel pretty and sexy. She looked around. Maybe someone she knew was watching them. Her husband was practically asleep in their booth, and her friend was dancing with one of the policemen. No one was paying attention. If only someone had, a decision wouldn't have been necessary.

"What do you say, Hon? Only for a little while." He leaned down and his lips were soft on hers, just a whisper of a kiss. The urgency in his voice thrilled and excited her. She felt the butterflies in her belly flutter, and the guilty pull of desire.

She let him dance her to the door… and out into the night.

# The Art of Cheating

there are some sins
worth committing,
and for far less than the benefit of fortune.
that one chance to cross the river
on a branch just two feet away.
and you don't close your eyes
or hold your breath, because
seeing and breathing are part of the sin.
you just board the plane
on a first class ticket
and spread the price
over time.

you invent a drama for
a well known friend
in a place that's hard to reach.
and you settle his suspicions,
the night before, by
pretending tonight's arms
are really tomorrow's.
and then just before
your guilt awakens
in righteous indignation –
you touch your lips
and remember –
that stolen kiss.

when you arrive,
overwhelm all of your senses.
touch. feel.
taste – a more exotic fruit.
maybe, something uncommon
to North America.
Polynesian, perhaps.
remember to entice and fascinate the mind.

speak on all your interest.
traverse the full perimeter
of that small portion
you are willing to share.
And soon you'll realize,
you've given it all.

now,
in a happened glance,
or a spark of glass
you'll see the
past that brought you here,
stalking
a forgotten dream.
and then just before
you speak on
absolution,
to acknowledge your carnal weakness –
again
remember –
to touch your lips.

feel their curvature,
their supple texture.
remember how a new warmth
traveled your body.
your chest, wrapped in
unfamiliar arms.
a cell eruption,
racing to your toes,
stopping between your legs along the way.
a sensation
along the crevice of your back.
those sudden surges of air,
oscillating you
back and forth through
consciousness.

you see,
there are some sins
never repented,
and for far less than the lack of condemnation.
that one taste of perfection
slowly seeping from the core.
and you don't close your hand
or cover  your heart, because
giving and loving are part of the sin.
you just board the plane
on a first class ticket.
and spread the price
over time.

# *Mirror, Mirror*

I have a mark beneath my left eye. My mother's sin is buried beneath it. A peculiar little scar blotched in no particular shape, marking the decades of my life. A life of lies, telling the story of a child never meant to be born. And in the dusty confines of our small attic closet, I found my picture – one day old. The mark is there at birth. My squinty brown eyes, innocent and blameless, are not yet carrying the burden of youth or beauty. My arms seemed to cuddle an invisible toy, content with the aseptic surroundings of this new world. The scar is much lighter there but it's still the same shape. I am told that it was a sign. A sign that God had forgiven my mother's sin.

\* \* \*

Her time for lye and poisons or hot water and hangers had long passed. Her belly was ready to burst. My mother's only hope was that sin and adultery would hide themselves. So in the harsh months of winter, she searched for absolution in a religious world where women only had one purpose. A child was a child, no matter whose child it was. But while the church offered confession, a magic lady offered hope. She told my mother, "bathe with this canister of herbs. Mix it in your palm with rose oil, then paste it across your body. Paste it heavy across the womb and between the legs. The water should be lukewarm. God will need both hot and cold to mark the soul of a child. Because children hold the promise of both love and despair. Sink down; keep the water above your shoulders and never *wipe* away the paste, for as the herbs slowly dissolve, so will the sin." She promised that God would send a sign and that no one would ever know. My mother's sin would be hidden and His true mercy would be inside the secrets.

It was my aunt Sue who found the magic lady. An old woman who lived at the end of Fort Greene. She'd been helping Miss Anna chase away her husband's mistress. That too required bathing and soaking. And it was my Aunt Sue who first noticed the mark. After they'd wiped me clean of blood and fluids, she whispered to mommy that God had indeed sent a sign. It was beneath my left eye.

Mommy gave the magic lady her last twenty dollars.

\* \* \*

In the winter of 1958, my mother worked nights at Doubleday. Daddy worked days at the navy yard steaming their lives through the surging sails of ships east and west. He made electronic triggers and wirings for bombs. She did typesets for the latest novels. Daddy's days passed slowly, filled with miniature maneuvers. But mommy's chatter filled nights moved quickly; hustling through pages and pictures. Women on the shop floor shared their bounty and heartache, their wisdom and fears. They shared remedies and potions for "female troubles." They filled each other's gaps when life *didn't* make ends meet.

And at the end of each day, the number 75 bus was there when they clocked out. My mother, my Aunt Sue and their closest friends wrapped in wool, faux fur and loyalty. Their river of dreams that flowed down Flatbush Avenue, seeking bridges and tunnels to downtown, hurried them through life – pounding their youth onto desolate banks. Only once in a spare pay, did the waterfalls gush down Broadway, Harlem or 125th Street. More often, their river of dreams receded in drought, ebbed on missed menstrual cycles or days of lust and liquor. Their lives were an endless tug of life against child, hope against marriage. That was the life of a child bearing woman.

My mother's struggle was rooted deeply in her quest to break free – free of the labels that held her back: mother of four, wife of one, leader of many. And she was smarter, sharper, quicker with numbers than any man she knew.

One time, she tried to get a clerical job assisting a young black CPA. He gave her a one week trial; had her taking notes at client meetings and answering his phone. She typed up a little business report he did for Mr. Dixon; the only black owner of a Key Foods Grocery. But when she found five mistakes in his math, he let her go. Said she didn't have the right voice for answering the phone. He kept Mr. Dixon's business though; saved him $300 dollars with the IRS – the same report my mother had typed up.

In late January, my mother's cousin Tee came to visit. Though the New York winter was only slightly milder than Michigan's lake side gust, Tee enjoyed a two week vacation from molding bumpers and welding hoods. Fred (Tee) Bowers was a second shift foreman at Ford's largest plant and he hadn't seen his favorite cousin in over two years. The children of dueling sisters, he and Mommy had forged a bond dating back to their youth. Finding their shared shame in neglect, they comforted one another during periods of abandonment, abuse and loneliness.

Tee's visit was like an emancipation for my mother. She took days off and partied in Harlem. Tee bought her a new dress. Fancy. The kind she could sashay in; strut down Prospect Avenue and make men rise. And Tee took her down every street he could find.

Daddy went out with them sometimes. He liked Fred Bowers. Tee was the only Thorpe family relative who hadn't shunned him. Unlike my mother's other relatives, Tee hadn't considered it a crime to take her away from her Detroit roots. Tee once said, leaving Thorpe Street gave my mother her womanly parts. Someday he would escape himself and find his own manhood. Cousin Tee was never married.

Most times, Daddy was too busy to go out with them. Not because of work; his days ended at 4 pm. Not because of his four sons; Miss Anna loved to watch them. But Daddy had other interests; a Mason's lodge he frequented three times a week, his longtime project to *build* our first TV and a sister who lived in Queens and needed help with her ailing husband; crippled in WWII.

Daddy was a serious man who only laughed twice in his whole life. I only knew two jokes. Most days he came home never wanting to talk or eat. He'd work in the living room until late night, inserting TV tubes, soldering wires and watching an oscilloscope – this magical box he never had the time to explain. Then finally, late into the evening, he'd eat from the lone plate on the back the of the stove, read the paper and fall asleep with his head against the wall. He seemed content with the sameness of life.

Tee spent his two week vacation exploring New York; a city he'd never seen. It was fuller and faster than Detroit, but Tee never seemed out of place. While my mother worked, he spent his time on Delancy Street or Flatbush Avenue. He discovered card games and Speakeasys; burlesque-like shows with black only casts. He'd start telling my brothers about these places, whispering the naughty parts. But Daddy would catch him and threaten him with one phrase; "if Sandy hears you…"

My mother and Tee spent their last Saturday night at a small club on Lenox Avenue. Mommy loved it there. Particularly because of the owner; a man name James Dabney. It was well known that Dabney had a "*thing*" for Mommy. She could get anybody in her party free drinks and a good table. He'd even extended his courtesies to Daddy once, when he and mommy partied together.

James Dabney was much older than Mommy; in his mid to late forties. He was born in Curacao. A very fair skinned West Indian man with hazel eyes and straight hair. He'd found success selling products to black salons throughout New York City. In the early fifties, he was the only supplier. It made him rich. He opened his first club just after his wife returned to Curacao. She didn't like New York; didn't like America; didn't like the company her husband kept.

Mommy's new dress fascinated Dabney and he was particularly generous to her that night. He gave Sue and Mommy orchid corsages. He opened a bottle of champagne for the table and offered Tee his good smokes. They sat center front. The best table to hear a new young singer do her versions of Lena, Sarah and Billie. When she stopped singing, the band played and everyone danced. Mommy danced with Dabney all night.

By one a.m., my mother and Dabney had slipped away. Tee and Aunt Sue drank, smoked and waited. There was no time limit on Mommy's excursion, she just couldn't come home alone.

The band did a final set at three, keeping the mood soft and quiet. Some listened, others simply dozed off. Jitneys waited outside for those who could manage to get to the door. But most sat quietly waiting for some portion of their buzz to wear off.

Mommy came back by five, her wilted corsage stuffed in her coat pocket. Though none of them were completely sober, my mother, Aunt Sue and Tee maneuvered through the slow running subway system and made their way back to Brooklyn. Aunt Sue slipped quietly into her apartment two flights up.

Tee's bus for Detroit left late the next evening. Daddy and Mommy both went to Port Authority with him. After a long goodbye, Mommy's tears and Daddy's handshakes, Tee returned to the world he knew and my mother returned to hers.

Daddy bought her a coffee in the terminal café. They sat and talked, watching new flakes sprinkle onto 41ˢᵗ Street. They seemed a pleasant couple, Daddy eagerly sharing his breakthroughs on building the TV. Mommy told him about the new singer at Dabney's – how she sounded so much like Sarah. Daddy said his sister would need him again next weekend, but he wouldn't leave until Saturday. Mommy said she'd make a dinner for him to carry.

The trains ran well that Sunday night, they were home quickly. After thanking Miss Anna for her usual good care, Mommy and Daddy went off to bed. He agreed to forego his other interest for one night.

\* \* \*

I was born late October of that year. Cousin Tee came back to visit. He brought Mommy some old pictures that Aunt Annie had saved for her. There were pictures of Mommy and Tee when they were young and even a few of Daddy. Annie wanted to know who I resembled. She made Tee promise to return with a picture of me. Even then, Annie had started her peculiar rumor that I was Tee's daughter; a result of his winter excursion. But Tee knew better. My dark hair, brown eyes and cocoa skin relieved his mind.

Tee showed everyone the pictures he'd brought from Detroit. A wedding photo of my mother and father and a studio portrait of them with my oldest brother, Vincent. He of course, is not the son of my father. He is the son of Vincenté Martialto; a Cuban man who had one-too-many wives. When Annie found out, she quickly had him "put" on a train to Canada; one way ticket in hand. The marriage was annulled and one year later my father officially adopted Vincent, Jr.

Curious thing about that picture; my brother and father looked more alike than any other child in the family. Same nose. Same eyes. They even smile the same. But I'm the only one with a mark. A peculiar little scar blotched in no particular shape. It's beneath my left eye, just like my father's.

## *A Proposition*

It was a dangerous but exciting place to visit in the mid-50's.
Tony and Rita were here in Greenwich Village, which attracted creative
free spirits and the bohemian, an atmosphere that exists even today.
Then, it was a myriad of arts and crafts; but the crime rate was high. That
didn't seem to stop people from attending the shows and music that
abounded there.

The couple was invited to an evening in New York by her aunt
and a gentleman friend, Frank, to celebrate Rita's birthday. Rita was
excited, for neither she nor her husband had ever been to the Village.
Frank was a nice guy; a little rough around the edges, with a strong city
accent. Once in awhile you might hear a 'dis'or 'dat' in his speech; this
surprised Rita, because he talked often about his college days. Little did
she know that 'college' was prison! Frank was wise in the ways of the big
city, too, and said there was a great stage show and a hilarious comedian
at a place called Club 54.

When the foursome arrived they settled down at a tiny table,
so small that their knees touched, and ordered a round of drinks. All
around them were beautiful people. It seemed as if the room was full
of celebrities, though Rita didn't recognize any one as being famous.
Most were in evening dress; Rita felt underdressed and out of place,
even though she wore her best beige and gold outfit, and best little pearl

earrings. Tony was handsome as ever in his good blue suit, white dress shirt and black tasseled loafers.

The waiters were overly solicitous; if you left the table one was right there to pull out the chair. When you returned, another would place your napkin in your lap. If you took out a cigarette, one would be there in your face with a lighter. They were four at the table, and there were two waiters hovering over them, at all times.

From the onset they seemed drawn to Tony; fawning, in fact. The servers were all very nice looking, dressed alike in navy suits, and all wore diamond pinky rings. If one of the four needed a refill, a waiter would turn to Tony, asking what *he* wanted. It was obvious that they were ignoring the other three. Rita got a little miffed, and Tony was fidgeting in his seat. "What the hell's going on with these guys?" he complained. Frank smirked and the aunt giggled. They absolutely cracked up when one of the waiters, a good-looking blond, handed him a playbill, and bending close to him whispered, "this is for our next show; hope to see you here." With a knowing grin he left the table, leaving the group slack-jawed, too shocked to say or do anything.

The comedian was also the emcee, and wished Rita a happy birthday; Frank had requested it beforehand, which thrilled her. The show, with its beautiful men and women all aglitter and sequined from head to toe, was truly entertaining. As Frank promised the comedian was extremely funny, though a bit raunchy for Rita's taste. At the show's end the players lined up onstage and exposed themselves to the audience, disclosing that the men were women, the women men, and everyone else was gay! Rita and Tony were amazed at the women who were guys, for they were stunning. One of them, a curvy brunette, stripped down to the bare facts and proved to be a man; Marilyn Monroe had nothing on him- her.

On the way home, a note fell out of the playbill that the cute waiter had given to Tony. He had surreptitiously slipped him a note with his name, address and phone number. "I can show you a good time." it said. A red-faced Tony blustered a few well-phrased epithets aimed at the blond. When Rita put two and two together, she laughed in glee, much to her husband's chagrin. "After all," she exclaimed, "you *are* wearing a navy suit, and your diamond pinky ring, just like the waiters.

No wonder the proposition! Everyone thought you were gay!"

# *Luce*

"Damn! Damn! Damn!" Luce ranted as she threw things into her overnight bag. Through the years she had learned to pack in a hurry and expertly. She could actually pack for three weeks in one carryall. "I'm getting tired of these Vegas trips. They're coming too often lately. To hell with reaching platinum status on the airline miles program." She threw on a red tank top, zipped her jeans with a hard yank and stepped into her Gucci red platforms. Her navy blazer completed the outfit. Casual was the dress of the day for traveling. As she looked around, Luce already missed her bedroom with its blue sateen sheets and royal blue comforter. She didn't look forward to the pricey but sterile hotel rooms of Vegas and the damn Hoover Dam! But her job included going where the organization sent her, and so she was on her way. . . again!

Steven was used to her frequent trips. They were the price for marrying an entertainment lawyer with an assertive attitude. Luce was damn good at her job and she knew it. It may bust the balls of the envious men in the company, but too bad! She loved Steve and they were comfortable with each other's life style.

Luce really minded leaving her boys for days at a time, for they were teens and needed their mom more than ever. She remembered her brothers' teen years, and the trouble young kids could get into. She didn't want her boys to follow in their footsteps. "Traveling was different when I didn't have them in my life, but now hopping back and forth has lost its appeal for me. I've seen it and done most of it," she mumbled to herself. Except for one enormous reason, Luce was tired of the yo-yo trips. She glanced around guiltily, as though someone might read her thoughts.

No one, especially Steve, knew about Marc Johnson. He was the only bright spot in all her journeys. A dangerous spot he was, too. Just thinking of him accelerated her blood pressure, and she felt the liquid rush, the warmth that spread through her. Luce still couldn't understand his attraction to her. Oh, she knew she was pretty enough, with her straight black hair and dark, almost jet black eyes. Blessed with a good body which she kept up by running each morning, and a fine sense of style, she could turn heads. And this specimen of a man, his unexpected electric blue eyes in that smooth, milk chocolate face was intent on seducing her. Wealth was written all over him; the button down Oxford shirts and tailor- made suits hung perfectly from those broad shoulders. "He must like tough women," Luce mused. She didn't realize that Marc saw through the no-nonsense facade to the softness underneath. She thought she hid that well, but the man was reaching for that very softness.

This was a drama that would never unfold on stage, or behind the scenes either, she knew; or rather prayed that she knew. She loved Steven and her boys, but who wouldn't be flattered by the attention from this self-assured peacock of a man? Luce had to deal with Marc business wise, though she was instinctively aware that he wanted more. The pressure of his hand on the small of her back as he showed her to the door sent shivers up her spine. An amused smile told her he knew the effect he had on her. The three hour lunches at the restaurant hidden away from the ordinary; hands 'accidentally' touching, the occasional knuckle sliding down the edge of her cheek; these were all signs of gentle seduction. When these things occurred, Luce wasn't sure that it was the Chardonnay that caused the flush in her cheeks.

The thought of another man besides her husband making love

to her was a constant turn-on, and the sinfulness of it excited her. True, marriage had become somewhat ho-hum after all the years, and the love was a 'of course I love him' sort of thing, but Luce couldn't wrap her mind around actually committing the deed. Tempting though it was, she shook her head determinedly. "I am definitely cutting these trips out," she declared. "Too much 'stressure' can kill." She hoped she had the will power to follow through on her promise. But oh, those eyes!

# *Let it Ring Once*

In Freeport, summer Saturdays always left me behind. Amidst the buzzing mowers and spit waxed convertibles, I was a poor black child with nothing to do. Summers were never spent abroad and traveling carnivals only visited two towns over. Our block was a maze of young men, living out their sports fantasies in the streets. Footballs and softballs hurled across the sky. Basketballs pounded the cement, echoing out our morning wake up call. The sounds of other young girls and slip slapping jump ropes was always too far away.

At times, sleeping in was the only remedy to a dull and lonely day. I would dream intricate fantasies of adulthood, mysterious journeys and knights in shining armor that rescued me from a mediocre life. A life that offered neither promise nor passion. On Saturday mornings letting go of the slumber world was even more difficult. There were no weekday morning chores to rise for. Mommy didn't need her dress ironed or her lunch fixed or my steady eyes to find her missing shoe. But when the sun crept through the Venetian blinds casting it's horizontal shadows, life and reality peeked through as well.

Though morning had just arrived, the house was already empty. My four older brothers had all left for summer jobs and sports camps. Mommy was out back, kneeling in her garden, shooing away blue jays who just wanted a taste. I moved around quietly, knowing that if she heard or saw my movement I would be beckoned outside to help. I didn't enjoy the weeding and planting and staking. Her tomato plants were high and her long distorted shaped cucumbers were ripe for picking. Evidence of a good summer already lined our kitchen. Sixteen ounce Ball jars, boiled and cooled, filled with pickled tomatoes, cucumbers, peppers, all crowded the kitchen table. Some were there for farm-like decorations. Others were lined up in rows, waiting for me to store them on basement shelves; our winter bounty; curing and delicious.

A rare breeze cooled the room and fluttered the handmade green and yellow curtains. I could still smell the evidence of Mommy's usual Saturday breakfast; eggs, grits and sausage. A feast she always cooked for one; fully aware of my disdain for hominy and eggs. Happily, she'd given up trying to get me to acquire her southern tastes.

She finally stood up surveying her progress, glancing behind her to re-check the sturdiness of her stakes and ropes. She caught sight of me standing at the kitchen sink. It only took her seconds to wave me over. "Did the phone ring," she asked? "Move it closer to the window so I can hear it, if it does." Her fingers pointed to the low bay window that nestled our tiny kitchen table. I nodded and headed back inside, hoping to avoid her bid to get dressed and come out to help. "And if it rings," she concluded, "don't answer." An instruction I'd become quite used to hearing.

She let me go back inside without her usual gardening request. She seemed pre-occupied with other plans. Plans that always involved her mysterious errand, preceded by the single ring call. I ate my cereal watching for the signal.

It came at 10 o'clock, just after Mrs. Armstead's Impala glided down the driveway. She and Mommy waved and shouted their pleasantries. She was off to the bakery and then to her women's club luncheon. Mommy promised to save her some homemade pickles and bring them by later.

Mrs. Armstead was a refined woman born in Japan; petite, polite, with dark brown eyes that saw inside you. Her small but meticulous rock garden was an odd concept for lawn bred Long Islanders. Tiny boulders

and moss and precision cut trees adorned her front yard; reminiscent
of ancient Kyoto. As a child, I wondered why she chose such an
uncommon landscape in a world of trimmed yews and weeping willows.
But I learned so much of her pride and grace, watching her tend her
garden. When Mommy got a job at Doubleday, Mrs. Armstead began
watching me when I came home for lunch. It was a world of fantasy.
Their fine home was like a museum; oil paintings and carved busts set
on marble columns and a grand piano all adorned their living room. She
would greet me at her door during my school time lunch breaks; tuna
sandwiches and hot chicken soup. And while I ate, she'd play Beethoven
and Bach, in a manner so grand, I could pretend I was a princess being
entertained by my court.

Mr. Armstead was an older man, black and from Detroit. I
used to wonder why Mommy didn't already know him since she was
from there too. But once I turned 9 and visited her old neighborhood,
I realized how big Detroit really was. And like Daddy, he was a WWII
veteran, but spent much of his Air Force career in big offices with big
generals. After the war, he spent time in Japan. Mrs. Armstead said he
was part of the United States' rebuilding team. He left years later with
new money and a new wife.

Mommy moved quickly after the single ring, removing her gloves
and tossing them on the back stairs. "If it rings again, don't answer," she
told me. But I already knew not to touch the phone.

She showered and changed; curled her hair and pinned it up.
Her attire was like work clothes; neatly pressed – like the oddity of
wearing your school clothes on a Saturday. But she slipped into flip flops
and rushed through the front door. I didn't dare come behind her, her
mere mannerisms were the command for secrecy. But she'd done this
far too many times for me not to wonder. I simply had to know where
she was going and now there were no big brothers around to stop me. I
glanced through the side window and saw her head up the street. But the
houses were so close, I couldn't see past the Armstead's house. I waited
a minute longer so she could get far enough away, but when I looked
out the front door, she was gone. I wondered how she could disappear

so quickly. I opened the door fully and stood on the steps, but she still wasn't there. I ran to the front curb and still couldn't see her. The phone rang again, startling me back inside. It only rang once.

I sat upstairs writing in my journal for the next hour; watching the neighborhood boys run back and forth, leaping for touchdowns and home runs. The summer noise had risen to a background hum one could easily ignore. But I heard the latching and rattling of the Armstead's fence. I looked out the window and saw Mommy gently closing and locking their gate.

# Recipes

# *A Ritual*

She sat in the middle of the kitchen like a queen. And we greeted her, "Como esta, Grandma." Then you got a taste of anisette, a clear liquor that Italians favor, alone or with black coffee, and even we children had to sip it, like it or not. It was all part of the ritual.

Sunday dinners started way back to my great-grandmother's time. Until she passed away at 94, every week consisted of attending church, Sunday school, and then going to Grandma's house for the day. We always went in the back door. I don't ever remember anyone entering the front door.

There were usually 12 people in attendance, sometimes more. I could never figure out how they all fit in that small space. One regulation size table with a long bench along the back wall, chairs squeezed seat to seat, a large wood burning stove with orange or apple peels smoldering on it, a heavy duty laundry sink in one corner, and a couch occupied this tiny kitchen! I never saw a refrigerator or ice box. It must have been hidden somewhere! There was no way for me to find out, because the rest of the house was off limits. I never saw the other rooms until Grandma died and was laid out in the living room.

The Sunday meal always began with chicken soup; Grandma's back yard was a breeding ground for chickens and ducks. A large German shepherd kept watch over the brood. Each week a hapless hen was sacrificed for dinner. After the soup came salad greens with a dressing of oil, vinegar and chunks of garlic. Pasta with meatballs and pork ribs followed. There was always a huge round loaf of crusty Italian bread. I don't remember having desserts. The grownups had wine with peaches soaking in a pitcher, and we children were given a touch of wine with orange soda. Every week my mother got tipsy on the wine and peaches, and had to go lie down on Grandma's bed, leaving me to do the dishes. After dinner a bowl of nuts was set out. We kids would bring ours to Uncle Joe to crack; he was missing one hand from birth, and he used the stump to crack open the nuts. At Easter time, our Uncle Nick, who was bald, would let us crack the hard-boiled eggs on his head. We had great fun doing these things!

When great-grandma died, my grandmother carried on the Sunday ritual, with a twist; the adults played cards before and after dinner. The menu was the same; salad, pasta, and chicken soup; Nonny raised chickens, too! Then it was back to playing cards.

We kids were left to fend for ourselves. There wasn't much to do, for Nonny's house was not equipped to accommodate children. We weren't allowed on the living room furniture, and because the adults played all night long, often until breakfast the next day, we would sleep on the rug in her living room. The only fun we had was rubbing our stockinged feet on the carpet and touching each other, causing an electric shock. There was no radio in the house, and television wasn't invented yet, so we either played word games, or did the carpet trick. We managed to keep ourselves occupied, or fell asleep purely from boredom.

When Nonny passed on, my mother took up the gauntlet. Sundays were held at our apartment – same menu, same company, same games. We children were older now, so we could leave after the three o'clock meal and go outside to play.

Thinking back, I don't remember anyone ever missing dinner. It seemed the meal was held in sickness and in health. Then my parents moved to Florida, leaving the rest of the family up north.

The ritual ended.

# How to Make A Meatloaf

A good meatloaf goes a long way. I should know. It's my one claim to fame in the culinary arts, that I make a good meatloaf. Now, I am a creative cook, a master of disguise and there was a time I even considered writing a cookbook for cheats.

Meatloaf:

Wait until the last minute to decide what to cook.

Take two pounds of frozen chopped meat out of the freezer and place on defrost in microwave.

Stop the microwave periodically to scrape off the meat that has started to defrost. Otherwise the chopped meat will begin to sizzle and it is difficult to mix hot chopped meat.

While defrosting, mix two eggs, a quarter cup of water, half a cup of Italian bread crumbs, half a cup of tomato sauce and my secret ingredient in a large bowl.

Take off your wedding, engagement and pinkie rings and if you are a messy masher, your watch. Never leave your diamond ring on the counter. This could possibly lead to someone swallowing a couple of karats.

Place diamond in safe container.

Take the now warm and slightly mushy chopped meat from the

microwave and blend with mixture.

There will probably be some still frozen lumps in the meat. I usually crush them in my hand, or just throw them in the damn mix.

While the oven is heating to 325 degrees, form a nicely shaped loaf out of the mixture, and cover with tomato sauce.

If you like you can grate some cheddar cheese, but I prefer to buy it already grated as I don't have that much patience when I cook.

After about twenty minutes sprinkle the cooking meatloaf with some cheddar cheese. If there is any tomato sauce left over, just slap it on the thing.

While the meatloaf is cooking scrub some baked potatoes and put a little oil on the skins. Pierce with a fork. Here you have several choices, to put the potatoes in the oven or the microwave. I believe in the best of both worlds. Zap them for about ten minutes, and then let them crisp out in the oven.

The meatloaf should stand for about ten minutes before slicing. It is important at this juncture to cover with a towel in case one of your cats or dogs decide to have a taste while you are setting the table.

Slice meatloaf and serve with baked potatoes and sour cream and a green vegetable or salad. Have the next day on rye bread spread with tons of mayo and a little ketchup. Have fried meatloaf that night with baked beans.

Keep smiling.

## *Meatloaf*

Meatloaf never liked me. I have tried more recipes for meatloaf than I can count.

Mother made the juiciest, most tasty meatloaf ever, and she taught me step by step how to duplicate it. It contained one and a half pounds of chopped meat, tomato sauce, two eggs, fresh green parsley, stale bread soaked in milk, with a slice of bacon on top to keep it moist. When she put it in the oven at 350 degrees, our big old, yellow linoleum kitchen smelled so good.

However, when I followed her instructions step by step, it was never the same. My family hated it! Though my children actually cried whenever I served meatloaf, I never gave up trying. I began receiving anonymous recipes in the mail. How anonymous could they be, the cowards! Whoever they were, they had to know me and my meatloaf. I tried them all, nevertheless; some called for onion soup mix, others for corn and peas, and still others for bread crumbs instead of bread. I took a stab at each and every one sent to me, without much success; my kids still cried. Knowledge of my failure was wide-spread.

Well, I finally found a recipe that my family didn't shed tears over. Yes, it was one of the anonymous suggestions. I was happily preparing meatloaf for company one evening, since I was now so proud of my new ability to do so. My menu consisted of crusty French bread,

101

creamy mashed potatoes, and crunchy green broccoli, with a Caesar salad. And my meatloaf sat snugly in the 350 degree oven.

I was washing my hands when I noticed that one of my pretty pink acrylic nails was missing. Though I looked desperately around the kitchen, I just knew it was in the meatloaf, lost as I kneaded the ingredients together. Was it fate, was my Karma bad? Now that I had found the perfect recipe, success eluded me. I know what it was; meatloaf simply never liked me.

We ordered out that night.

# Vows

## *My Wedding Day*

A week before the wedding I'm sitting on a step stool in our large yellow tiled kitchen in the house on Cottage Place. My mother brandishes a large pair of scissors. I'm preparing myself for something I haven't had in years; a haircut. My brothers are sitting at the table admonishing me. "Don't do it, Rita." But the scissors move and they watch sadly as inch by inch of my life's growth floats to the floor, to be swept up and thrown away like dust bunnies under a bed. I feel light-headed. The fact that I lost an integral part of me is overwhelming; my tears well up for Tommy, too, who sits looking forlornly at the floor where my crowning glory now resides. My ponytail is gone and my mother puts her glasses on to see how she did, a scary habit of hers.

"It feels strange, Mom." "It looks good," she says calmly, "Go look in the mirror."

I like my new pixie haircut; it's right in fashion with the stars this season. Ava Gardner, Liz Taylor and Audrey Hepburn are sporting the new 'do's. Except for Tommy and Junior everyone else seems to like it.

My bridesmaid is cajoling. "You have to wear a little lipstick, you'll be wearing white; you're too pale." So I suffer the indignity of having someone put lipstick and a little rouge on my bare face. I'm not used to wearing make up. The closest thing to me wearing make up was from the little candy store on the way to school; I would buy 'red hots' and rub one on my lips, making them pink.

I slip into my peau du soire silk gown with the scalloped hem and set the little silk cloche hat with the lacy veil on my head. My future mother-in-law has given me her pearl necklace; it looks perfect, each creamy pearl graduating in size to form a perfect circle around my throat. The bridesmaids, all five of them, are oohing and aahing as I stand in front of my bedroom mirror, looking at a strange girl staring back at me. Could this be the tomboy who hates wearing dresses?

"Don't be nervous," one girl says. Another chimes in, "I'd be a nervous wreck, but look at her-she's calm as a clam." Yeah, right. I turn, run into the bathroom and promptly throw up. Everyone screeches; hands are all over me; who's holding my head, who's keeping my gown from the unpleasantness. Now I must brush my teeth-again, apply lipstick-again, look calm-again. The gown is v-necked and I have red blotches over my neck and chest. So much for calm.

Downstairs we all go. To the living room to take pictures. Mom has done her Italian thing, as her mother before her and her mother before her has done. Aunt Ange, Uncle Nick, assorted cousins; all have red and green living rooms, covered in thick plastic; heaven forbid a spill or a stain! Mother's pride has forced her to re-cover the old set that traveled with us from Newark to the Jersey shore nine years ago. This is her only concession to my wedding day. There isn't even a tray of cookies for relatives who come from out of town.

"Mom, usually the family puts out something to nibble on, in case people come early. You know how Uncle Sammy looks for food the minute he walks in the door."

"What for? We'll be going right to the church soon." I bit my tongue in shame. I knew there was no money for extras this day.

Pictures taken; artificial poses in front of the mirror; me looking at me, wondering who that is in a wedding gown, looking scared as hell.

As we leave for Saint Michael's my mother, needle in hand follows, still sewing the hem on her handmade lavender dress. Someone stops short- "Ouch!!" She stuck Alicia in the arm with the needle.

"Geez, Mom, shouldn't that have been finished earlier?"

"Sorry, she stopped too quick." It is a pretty dress, she's a good seamstress; I didn't get that talent from her. And Alicia's not bleeding, so life goes on.

"Daddy, you look John Garfield handsome in your tux."
"Mmmmm," his only response. He made me cry for days, threatening not to wear a tux. Dad isn't used to dressing up casual, no less in a tuxedo. Time to go; there are no limos waiting for us; we have friends driving the wedding party to the church and the reception. We're lucky Dominic has a white car; that's for me and Tony.

Saint Michaels' church is a beautiful old red brick building, across the street from a lake. Inside a lovely pink, lavender and purple décor, the stained glass filtering pretty colors into the room and onto the crowd. I've been attending services here since I was eleven years old, and here I am going to marry my childhood sweetheart at its altar. A very peaceful feeling comes over me. It doesn't last long...

There's a crowd outside the church. I'm thinking they're thinking, *We'll believe it when we see it!* No one thought I was right for Tony- we are the Rebel and the All-around Handsome Athlete, an incongruous couple. Inside the pews are filled with family and friends, none of whom I recognize in my nervous state. The tall, strapping ushers have seated the people. The Wedding March begins; the bridesmaids in their shrimp-hued gowns precede me. Now it's my turn.

I'm holding onto Daddy's arm for dear life. Am I really going to take this very big, very important step? We manage the mile long aisle, while I'm hoping nobody knows how my knees are shaking. Dad reaches to lift my veil, to kiss me goodbye and give his only daughter away to another man. He bunches the veil atop my head and I hear a sob catch in his throat. I hug him tightly, whispering, "Cut it out, you'll make me cry." My maid of honor straightens the veil and I hand her my bouquet of baby orchids and baby's breath. Here we go, ready or not!

As we're kneeling at the altar, the solemnity of the occasion is interrupted; we hear snickers and light laughter coming from the spectators. Not able to turn around and see why, Tony and I look at each other, puzzled, then shrug it off. Later we learn his younger brother Joey printed HE - LP on the soles of Tony's shoes.

It's over, it's official- I am now Mrs. Anthony Louis Santos! Holy Cow!

The voice of our friend Kate singing 'Ave Maria,' follows us down the aisle and out of the church.

Our reception is being held at the Deck in Belmar, a popular place for such occasions. It's an old but distinguished looking building with a beautiful deck overlooking the river. The bar on the first floor is a meeting place for young and old. I wouldn't know-I'm not old enough to drink yet! I admire the gray wooden structure with its worn wooden floors gleaming with polished care. *Good choice!* I think to myself as we enter the wide double doors.

The guests are coming upstairs to the dining room. Uncle Al slips, falls, splits his head open and an ambulance is called. Look-everyone just walks around him! They look with pity, but they walk wide to avoid the blood. Hard to believe my eyes! Could this be a sign of things to come? I hope not.

It's the hottest day of the year, though it's October of 1954. The women are wearing their furs, and vainly refuse to remove them in spite of the heat. Tony's Aunt Mary passes out. The owner announces over the microphone, "Please remove your jackets or coats. The air conditioning is not working and it's close to eighty degrees in here." Thank God for deodorant! But the furs were beginning to get a little gamey, too. No air; another omen?

My new mother-in-law is in a panic. "We can't have Father Celentano sit at the head table." "Why not?" we ask puzzled. "He'll be number thirteen, bad luck!" These 'signs' are beginning to worry me. So we move the good Father to her table, which she probably wanted in the first place, and everyone breathes a sigh of relief.

Daddy's little girl dances to 'Daddy's Little Girl', and Mommy's little boy dances to 'Sonny Boy', which happens to be her nickname for him. By now everyone is having a good time dancing, so we pay Rocky for another hour of twisting and doing the 'monkey.' He obliges.

Noises coming from the deck prove to be an inebriated Bob and Rich throwing chairs into the river. We never should have had an open bar. The bill will have an added cost of $12.50 each; four drowned chairs. Damn them, anyway!

When the time comes to leave the frivolity, I'm shown to a room downstairs to change into my street clothes. "In there," the waitress says, points to a small dressing room, turns and goes back upstairs. I'm in no hurry to change into the heavy black and white wool suit, more suited to the cooler weather than the sweltering heat outside. My stockings are ruined from dancing, and I don't have another pair. All of a sudden I panic- there's no one to help me undo the gazillion satin covered buttons on the gown that travel from my neck to my behind. The room is off the main bar, so I stick my head out to see if I know anyone out there. Thank goodness; Tony's Uncle Carmen is at the bar, so I commandeer him to unbutton me. This takes awhile for Carmen has had much libation. At last, here I am in my very warm suit with no stockings on, a little worse for the wear. And too late after the fact, wedding planners were born!

We are about to pay the bill; this is the 'hold your breath and hope we have enough money' time. Tony and I are depending on cash gifts, which we need to pay for the pleasure of this lovely party. We fervently hope the envelopes' contents will cover the expense. Neither of our parents can afford this wedding, though most of the guests are theirs. If *his* mother invited fifty people, then, by God, *my* mother had to have just as many, sneaking in a few more, even. Mom opens the cards and writes who gave what in a little book that I'll later use to write thank you notes. I don't believe Uncle Frank gave us a mere five dollars! He brought his wife and three kids, though the invitation said "no children please." The nerve!! After the bill is paid, we're thrilled that we have five hundred dollars left; we can buy a stove and fridge for the apartment, which didn't come with appliances. What if we didn't have the money for them? What would we have done? I break into a sweat thinking about it. Or maybe it's just the damn suit.

When I think about how we managed this whole affair by the seat of our pants, I wonder what the hell were we thinking? But things turned out well, meaning without a death or a shooting, and this is a good thing. We say goodbye to our parents and bridal party, climb into our 1952 gray Chrysler convertible and go off to conquer Florida...

Tomorrow the world!

# *Slipcover*

A majestic green collage,
this tapestry of shades and textures,
it's never been touched—

my mother's couch, covered in plastic,
since the day she brought it home.

Three swirling greens,
unfolding upon themselves
needled through a copper ridge,
bolted between mahogany
or pine stained as such.

Now uncovered,
bare beneath the eye –
and suddenly you wonder,
what was she protecting?

# *Going Once*

Pompous looking sheath,
studded in powdered pearls,
waltzed down the aisle just once —
my sister's wedding dress was piled
for second hand auction, the day she divorced.

Silken, layered, embroidered,
a blinding white hypocrisy.

Puffed up in pride and virtue,
wishing it could squeeze just
one more bosom into wedded bliss.

Stiff, standing
on its own without a hook.

My sister,
caressing the veil,
then trying it on –
blushing,
as though she'd never worn it.

## *Morning Silence*

He was still snoring, only eight thirty two a.m., but the street was waking up, making noise. The garbage truck just went by and she could hear Ally across the street greeting someone as she left to drop her boys at pre-school. Patsy concentrated on the sounds. There, she heard a bird, a soft chirp, a tap, tap, of a hammer, the whistle of the train, and soon, she knew she'd hear the nine o'clock bells. There were two belfries in town, each rang the hour but never together, as if they had a musical agreement to ring sequentially. So, the hour always struck twice.

A cough, rumble in the chest. Tom had stopped smoking a year ago after fifty years of one, then two, then three packs a day, chain after chain, then nothing, but the residue, the cough. Soon he would be up. She needed the morning, alone with her energy, her focus before their tango of togetherness began, its close steps a suffocating rhythm of parry and retreat, compromise or not.

Their marriage had become a delicate two-step. There were days when they worked in harmony. Tom doing repairs on projects around the house. Patsy finding a corner to write or make a phone call. Tom organizing paperwork in the office. Patsy stripping the sheets, weeding the garden, going for a walk. But it could erupt at any moment into a downward spiral of mutual annoyance.

The mindless tedium of everyday chores flared into

confrontation, simple stupid things like the proper way to hang a picture, or change the kitchen garbage bag. Tom said she didn't tighten it properly around the rim, and she'd acquiesce for it was hardly worth an argument. He told her once when she was damp mopping the hardwood floor she was using the wrong sponge mop. This and the proper way to clean a microwave oven had become fodder for jokes with friends whose husbands had retired. They'd share their piques, roll their eyes, and laugh too loudly, shrugging their shoulders at the inevitability of it all.

Tom was quick to anger, always had been. Flash, flare, and then over as if his rage did not impact on another human being in his way. He knew this about himself and worked on it, but it was a strong strain so ingrained he often seemed "surprised" if he offended someone.

Patsy cultivated a colorful flower garden around the borders of their small backyard and enjoyed arranging bouquets. One day as she snipped stems, pulled off straggly leaves and kept the flowers damp in the kitchen sink, she walked away for a few minutes. Then she heard a loud, angry yell, "God damn it!" "What's going on?" she asked as she walked back into the kitchen. And there he stood like an angry child, lashing out, crazy loon, yelling, "I am so sick and tired of finding your garbage in the sink. For Christ's sake do you want to plug it up with all these leaves?" At first, she was so incredulous; she just stood there, mouth agape, speechless. When her anger came, she was in a rage, a rage that his childish behavior interrupted a serene moment, a silent moment all to herself. She pushed him. She actually pushed him! "Do you think I'm some kind of f---- idiot? Stay out of my stuff. It's my stuff, not yours. You have enough Goddamn crap and junk in this house for ten men. Worry about that!" He backed off, dumbstruck, but she was shaking. He had just simply gone too far, in a moment laced with anger beyond her understanding. She couldn't fix it, but she could disallow it. The quiet reverberated around the scent of roses and zinnias as Patsy, turning her back to him, breathed deeply and picked up a stem.

Tom had a nice smile, a little boy smile that drew you in like a kid with a stolen cookie. He kept it tucked away behind serious eyes that often seemed focused on a distant place, a private place. To Patsy it seemed like he was swimming in a pool of darkness she could never reach, an island of negative energy that often drew her in and slowed her natural rhythm. She would ask, "Tom, are you alright?" and his answer was always the same, "I'm just thinking." Tom would go through downward spirals and she always saw them coming, the first uncomfortable sign when his eyes focused on nothing.

She would watch, and worry and wonder and wait, wait for the light to come back, his presence to appear and then there he was.

He was the baby of his family, the youngest of six children. Perhaps being born during the Depression to a large family colored his manner. He accumulated enough tools and ladders and gadgets to supply the neighborhood, and he did. "Ask Tom, he's got one of those." The attic was crammed with boxes of paper work and cancelled checks and three ring binders that would never be opened again. He was a hoarder and did not like to throw anything out. This would get to Patsy, for he was always reclaiming things from the garbage, a regular Robin Hood of refuse.

Tom was always home. She wasn't. There were days when she would be gone for hours and hours, meeting friends for lunch, going to a class, sometimes away for twenty four hours visiting a girlfriend. She wanted him to go away for a while, to leave her to stare at the walls, or manicure her toes, or wash the floor.

And yet, they still shared camaraderie, uniqueness as a couple who had struggled to survive. People who spent time in their company liked them together, enjoying their deprecating wit, their easy conversation and intelligence.

But Patsy's nerves were on edge today. Her daughter said her own artistic temperament was a "finely tuned instrument." Patsy understood that, and she knew that her own instrument had been sheathed in the burlap of the exigencies of life. Inch by painful inch she was slowly peeling the burlap off, revealing the pink, raw creative skin. She would tell him that she needed a few hours this morning, and he would be fine with that. But it still grated on her, the need to explain, to ask, to liberate a space just for her.

The belfries rang ten, then ten again. She heard the water running, then the toilet flush in the upstairs bathroom. Her jaw tightened. "I can do this," she thought. "I can keep my energy for me today, it's all in my head." Then she heard his footfall on the stairs.

\*\*\*

Their marriage had been one of absence. Tom in Africa, or Guatemala, Panama, Washington, Florida, even Brasilia with his job at

ABC News. He shared goat piss with a tribal chief, got a lung infection from bat caves, met Presidents and astronauts, lived on the edge. She created a support system of women with husbands on the road, women married and yet alone, strong, independent women who would gather the children for pot luck suppers and sleepovers, who sipped wine from a bottle of cheap Chablis, soothing tears, refereeing fights, cutting up strawberries for short cake.

His cough, his footsteps rang the bell of her memory. When he came home from an assignment the sense of absence still existed, as the chasm of their very different lives widened. He'd stay in his workshop in the garage, or watch a football game. She'd curl up on the couch and read. They never had to pass each other in the big house, isolated yet together. Now they were bound in an old Victorian cottage by the sea, all chintz and teal blue walls, riots of flowers on a friendly porch, prisms of light through stain glass windows, rooms with little space where elbows brushed and corners crowded when the day felt tremulous. But it was a good place, a place where neighbors visited on their porches, where people of different ages, races, and persuasions joined in common kindness. Tom had blossomed here, bantering when he was in a good mood, or acting the curmudgeon that he kidded he'd become. For so many years in the house on the hill he had been removed, out of touch, unaware of the rhythms of the street, the changes as the children grew, the suburban routine. Old friends said, "He's blossomed."

She had carved out a small space for herself with a bright red painted desk where she could write, and close the door, and it often felt like a selfish act instead of a liberation, an ownership of herself. It was cool today. She felt the chill breeze coming through the screen.

Tom was outside sweeping leaves from the buck eyed maple trees and she heard him chatting with a neighbor, Jim, a funny guy who called up to the window, "Hey, Patsy, you in there?"

Patsy called out the window, "You makin' trouble again, Jim." "Just keepin' tabs on the old guy," he answered.

"So far, so good," she thought. In the distance she heard the whistle of the 12:46 train. Soon the chimes would ring.

\* \* \*

Patsy wished she could stop thinking about dinner. It was always there, everyday, gnawing, nagging, intruding, the old tape of domesticity that runs on and on in a constant loop, stifling. She had to shrug it off.

Tom was very relaxed about food; content with a tuna fish sandwich, a bowl of spaghetti, or a last minute Chinese take out, but the process of just thinking about it distracted her. Even simple fare required thought, rye bread for the tuna, sauce and Italian bread for the spaghetti. She always stocked up on things he liked, a bucket of chicken, Cheeze-itz, peanut butter. He'd sit down with a couple of chicken wings and a few slices of cheese for a late lunch and watch re-runs of NYPD Blue or Law and Order. He was really self-sufficient. This week he had an infected tooth extracted and went about making soft boiled eggs and soup. And yet each day Patsy felt she needed a plan for the evening meal.

During the years that he was away on assignments he'd always arrive home with a bevy of leftover things from the television trailer, spatulas and can openers, Corning Ware and crock-pots. He liked stuff. Patsy never got the hang of those crock-pots. Other moms would be ecstatic about how they sliced up green peppers and beef, onions, tomatoes, potatoes at 7:00 A.M. for the six o'clock meal. She tried it once and thought it was ridiculous to be so focused on something eleven hours away.

Tom occasionally fixed something for dinner. He made great burgers and liked to toast up BLT's. It was such a lovely feeling, a comfort, a small hiatus to be served a sandwich while watching Jeopardy. They were both good at Jeopardy and she would often surprise herself at the obscure answers that rose to the surface of her mind. Tom played like a little kid waiting for a pat on the back, looking over at her, chuckling to himself, watching her response, "That was a good one, Tom."

\* \* \*

On a rainy day last week they had watched an afternoon movie together. It was that odd time of the day, four o'clock when time is in limbo, the events of the day slowing fading in the routine of sameness as the perching evening awaited. Patsy brewed coffee and put her restless mind on hold, and they sat together in soft comfort as the day waned, and the rain shivered on the windows.

The movie was one of their favorites, a sweet film made in 1988 "Rocket Gibraltar," with Burt Lancaster. An ageing grandfather of a large brood of kids, he quietly passes away in his room as the family is preparing a lavish birthday party in his honor. He often told the children the tales of the Vikings, and how when a Viking died they put his body

in a boat, set it on fire with a arrow, and let it drift out to sea, back to
nature. When the children discover he is dead, they decide to give him
a Viking funeral.  So they take him to the ocean, rig up an old boat, set
it adrift and on fire as their parents chase them all over the dunes of the
Hamptons. Tom had often said, "That's what I want, a Viking funeral."

The movie made Patsy cry for them both. She thought they may
never have grandchildren who'd remember them.  It was a reminder that
they needed to make arrangements for their deaths, to tie up the lives
they led in an urn or a coffin.  Tom was to be cremated, but Patsy was
still ambivalent since the Catholic Church lifted its ban on cremation.
She didn't particularly like the idea of being in a box in the ground, but
then she didn't want to be a box of bones in someone's closet, either.  She
thought it would be nice to have her remains thrown into the ocean, but
someone told her that it was illegal.  She said, "Oh, who the hell would
know, for Christ's sake?" After all, once they got Tom in that fiery boat a
few extra ashes were nothing.

She heard the whirr of a helicopter and the low drone of a small
plane flying over the ocean. The crisp white air fluttered through the
screen, carrying the mysteries of the other side of the sea.

Patsy was truly grateful they had found their way here, where
windowed doors opened onto sidewalks and shops, where music filled the
summer nights, where deep breaths of salt air cleansed the rough edges of
everyday.  It was a place to learn how to be with each other as the sand in
the hourglass of life dwindled.

Her neck and shoulders felt tight.  It was time to close up shop
for today.  The afternoon sun cozied up to the red and white pillows on
the futon, inviting her to snooze in its warmth like a drowsy cat.  Then
Tom called up to her, "Hey, Patsy, feel like a walk into town for a coffee?"
She called back, "Sounds great, be right down."

As they strolled toward the east, arm in arm, the sun at their
backs in the mid- afternoon, the chimes rang three, then three again.

# The Beach

Feet warm,
softly coddled
mounded  arch,
on sands of silver gold.

Eyes closed,
ears wide open
roaring splash,
thunder waterfall of ocean.

Body prone,
skin to
flying breeze
of billowed breath
oh ancient font of sea.

Breathe of
scented salt
Poiseden's musk
Pores to the sun in solitude,
alive.

# *Mosaic*

### *The Rain*

     I came to this place for the poor, the homeless, the addicted one-month after my last drink. I came on an icy January day, holding tightly to the wrought iron railings around the old stone convent, the once stained glass windows gone, replaced with heavy Plexiglass. I came for a two-week temporary job assignment. My once deep dug roots of success and striving, even my degree at age forty-six, the battles for power, the self importance were whittled down by my struggle with alcohol. And although I was fifty years old, I was just a girl who typed like a demon and still could write in that arcane language of shorthand.

     As I slid down the street late for my little job, perhaps I wondered why I fought the elements that morning, driving through the sleet to the dark inner city. It would have been a simple thing to call the agency and withdraw from the assignment, especially on such a dangerous day. Windblown and wet I held the icy railing on the red brick steps, took a deep cold breath and opened the door.

     A fellow in his thirties behind a beat up metal desk brought me into the office, the former chapel, now painted a drab tan and crammed with desks and printers and cheap glass partitions. The office manager settled me at my desk, and I was informed that the boss, "The Monsignor" would be there soon. What the hell! A Monsignor?

He blew in like a force of nature. A man in his sixties, very tall, over six feet, vibrant, life filled and on a mission, always in motion, joking in Spanish to the bookkeeper, barking orders, his size 12 red high top sneakers carrying him through his domain. Off he went to the soup kitchen to get the people out of the rain; up to the halfway house, down the street to the shelter, across to the courthouse to corral an alcoholic with a DWI.

We sat in his small crammed office. His dictation was fast, very fast and every few minutes he said, "Did you get that?" And off I went, half memory, half notes to type up the letters. We got along. He said, "Thank goodness they finally sent someone with a brain." Soon I was stepping in with other endeavors. Writing press releases, rewriting a grant that was a mess. He began taking me to meetings, "Grab your coat, I have to shake up those people at Human Services." He was a fighter. He wanted more space, bigger buildings, more services and money for the people in his care.

When my two weeks were up he asked me to stay. I was tentative. Did I really want a job in this dingy office in a questionable neighborhood, working on an old electric typewriter and a computer from the dark ages? But I also felt the energy, the promise, the purpose, and the safety, the safety from men and women who spoke the language of addiction and cared for each other. And Monsignor had a vision, a vision to build and grow and expand this mission to the poor, the sick and the addicted, and he wanted my help.

Five years later Governor Christine Todd Whitman came to the ground breaking of our six million dollar complex with shelters, halfway houses, a free clinic and a dining room that served 250 poor people a day.

I had heard him color the story of the day we met over and over again at fundraisers and galas and dinners. Each time the drama escalated. He told of a nervous, troubled woman who came for a two-week job. He told of how he saw beyond to my creativity and discovered my "brilliance." He told of how he hired me and made me Development Director. And I would stand up in a room of 500 people and take a bow. The story was not really about me. It was about his belief in the mosaic of life, the mystery of how the pieces fit and become a large and beautiful design.

And then, he saved my son's life.

## *The Recovery*

He was electric blue lightning from the first, born ten minutes after twelve on Leap Year 1968. If he could he would have walked home. That is my J.R, the beautiful boy with energy, daring, the irrepressible cowlick of brown hair on his forehead, the twinkling and mischievous brown eyes. At four months old he had a seizure, and when his little body was hooked up to the EKG machine, they said everything looked fine.

He did everything early and was determined to get up and walk before his first birthday. His reputation for daring began when he was two or maybe three, his trike wandering off the safe path of our apartment complex to ride down a flight of stairs, so quick that even a mother's steady gaze could slip up. He was smart and funny and a little too peppy for some teachers, hyperactive they said, but then ADD was not a common phrase in the lingo of child rearing.

At thirteen his voice changed, and he changed, the positive energy turned inward, secretive, self-destructive. The childhood pals were replaced by the slick and stealthy. The tuning fork of his life became discordant and the discord grew louder, damaging the bright, brilliant boy, and then the man.

When the call came from the woman who loved him the police had taken him to the hospital for he was drunk and suicidal. I could get no information. The Monsignor who was able to go anywhere with his status as a priest and a champion of the downtrodden, stepped in. The hospital wouldn't keep him for he had no insurance so he brought him to his house and kept him there for three days while he detoxed from alcohol. On the fourth day he was admitted for treatment, a free one year rehabilitation program.

I was in my office at my desk when he brought J.R to admitting. Discretion was important, but they let me see him before he began the first phase of treatment, a three month period of intense counseling with limited contact with family and friends. His hair was long and stringy and his head was bowed. He wore an army fatigue jacket and a flannel shirt, workboots on his feet, a duffel bag in his hand. As I put my arms around him I said, "You're in the right place." And he knew. He knew that all the years of trying to stop drinking, of all the long conversations, the threats, of all the missteps and bad decisions, he could choose to live. I watched his back as he was escorted down the hall, my mother's heart beating for him, my allies in this place of hope nearby.

### The Ring

The diamond solitaire in a platinum setting was my Mom's, nestled in a velvet box for seventeen years since she died. In all that time I had resisted suggestions of having it reset, or placing the diamond on a chain around my neck. I now knew where the ring belonged. When J.R left the halfway house four years before he had nothing but a dark rented room in the basement of a house, a job and a ride to it. Then the arc of his recovery broadened and he rode each uphill curve with patience, dignity and a devotion to the Blessed Mother ignited by his love for "Nana."

And so on a warm summer day I offered him the ring whenever he wanted it. He said, "Mom, this is a very old and valuable ring," and we spoke of my parents and the past and that yes, the ring was over eighty years old and the family all agreed that Nana would want him to have it. With a shy hesitation he said, "Can I take it now?" and another chapter began.

The old stone chapel in the woods was dressed for a celebration, its weathered wooden doors smothered with green and white hydrangeas, cascades of satin ribbon marking each pew, white candles on the sills and on the altar. The Monsignor, now in his eighties, but still an imposing figure, stood in his white robes as they prepared to take their wedding vows. They glowed with the light of the reborn, he in his tuxedo, his eyes bright, his back straight, sure and confident; her gown shimmering beneath the wisps of her long blonde hair, she, the woman who never wavered through his darkest days. The Monsignor spoke eloquently, even managing to mention ever so slightly the story of how we met and how the final piece of the mosaic begun that day. The diamond ring on her finger was not reset to reflect the fashion of the times, its timeless luster just polished to a new light, the solitaire bound once again to a platinum wedding ring.

Soft guitar music ushered the bride and groom and their guests out to the warm crystal September day. As Tom and I waited on the hill below the chapel greeting our guests the newlyweds appeared at the top of the stairs to many shouts of joy.

The rose, aqua, green and gold of the stained glass windows sparkled in the sun under boughs of green. The rough pink stones of the chapel steps framed her white gown and his dark tuxedo. The guests in festive attire lent speckles of brightness to the scene. As I pictured the moment in my mind's eye it formed a perfect mosaic.

# *Who Are You?*

Who are you? I sense your presence beside me
You shadow me, you walk my walk
I talk, you listen carefully

Do you know me? I think you do
Who are you? I feel you always
Why are you here? I wonder at the thought

That I may lose my mind
And you will still be here
Listening with care. Who are you?

Should I scream, you hear
But never leave my side
I sleep – you tend me still
Who are you? Stay by me ever.

# Branches

---·•✦•·---

# *Aunt Alice*

Of all the family who lived on Dixon Street, Nana, Pat, Raymond, Eileen, Alice and Aunt Mary next door, Alice had a "problem" that manifested itself in odd ways. She had a mental illness and was quite paranoid, and although both friends and family knew this it was not discussed openly. It was not an era of openness and awareness of emotional disorders, nor were the miracle drugs for psychosis available as they are today. My nana would whisper, "She's had the divil in her since she was a little one," and my mother absolutely forbade my brother and I from ever commenting on the episodes of rage and hysteria that we witnessed. When she had a nervous breakdown and had to be sent away for a while, it was a fuzzy thing we didn't know much about, but I cannot forget those strange days with Aunt Alice.

She always wore white Ked sneakers and little white anklets, and on a good day she would stand on her tippy toes in those sneakers and dance like a ballerina. There were stories about Alice to rationalize her behavior. She wanted to be a nurse like my mother, but she was allergic to chemicals. She was very beautiful as a young woman and quite sought after, but never found a match. My father's friend, Johnny Friel, was madly in love with her, but she didn't think he was good enough for her. When I was about ten years old something terrible did happen to her when she was hit on the head and robbed one evening. This sort of trauma is devastating to a well-balanced person, but it became a vindication of how people were out to get her, and exacerbated her illness.

She had a great affection and love for me and my brother, but it was uncomfortable to be alone with her, as sometimes she would go into her world of stories about the people spying on her. "That mailman can't fool me. He's just watching, wants to read my mail. I heard them whispering. They think they can fool me, giggling in the back, checking out my groceries, waiting to see what poor Alice is having for supper."

The really sad thing about her was she was the most generous person, and worked feverishly in that house, scrubbing, cleaning, and cooking. In the evening after dinner, the breadboard would come out and she would prepare lunch for Raymond and Pat for the next day, a routine that she'd accomplish with silent whispering under her breath. She had worked for a while, but had to stop, as she was fearful and exhausted.

Her eyes were hazel and they had intense shine that would fiercely focus on you, and you could never say "no" to Aunt Alice but acquiesce to her determination on giving you tissue wrapped packages from her room, pieces of red and white mint candy, a package of embroidered hand towels, a box of cracker jacks, packets of sachet, or from the pantry boxes of graham crackers. On the surface this might seem like fun, but this was born of an insistence that sometimes would go on for a long time, and she ran up and down the stairs while we were held hostage.

Aunt Alice was very particular about where she sat on the beach. When she came to the beach with us we had a long wait while she got ready. We whined a lot, "Can we go now?" "How much longer?" We were firmly told be quiet and just wait. When she was ready and we all set out, the next phase had to be negotiated but it never was. She always got her way, much to our consternation. Now, there was a group of women from the neighborhood who always sat in the same spot on the beach, near our favorite place to swim, where all our friends were. But Alice refused to pass them. They would "talk about her." so we had to sit at the very other end.

My mother was always kind and sympathetic to Alice and expected us to comply with her wishes and not make a fuss. Aunt Eileen and Uncle Pat were the only people who could handle her, especially when she would fly into rages. They had the strength to challenge her and she would back down. Mom and Ray were the pacifiers. I know Ray would pray for her.

Although she always attended all family events, weddings, christenings, barbecues, get-togethers her life was very limited by her illness and she was never able to participate in the world at large, to work, to travel, set goals, have a girlfriend. I saw her shortly before she died at the age of eighty-three from cancer of the liver. God has spared her pain in the end and she went quietly. But, the last time I saw her in the kitchen on Dixon Street, she still wore her white Keds, and her eyes still compellingly held mine. She was Godmother. I wish her peace in heaven.

# *The Man*

He was the baby of the family, one of eight children, all born within the first fourteen years of the Twentieth Century, the last to be born and the last to die. He lived all his life in a white house with green shutters on a narrow little street in downtown Newport, RI. with Alice, Eileen and Patrick, his other single siblings.

When he died on Memorial Day weekend, it seemed fitting for a man who lived a quiet life, but one to be remembered. The gift of his life shined with humility, humor, kindness and a deep intelligence he carried like an invisible cape, never boastful when his Irish eyes would twinkle with the sagas of the kings of Ireland, or the last of the Plantagenants, or the Latin names for the magnificent flowers in his garden. Born into the Greatest Generation who served in World War II, he never spoke of the battles he fought only that he had a furlough in Paris.

The day of his wake, his nine nieces and nephews stood in the receiving line. Some of his twenty-five great nieces and nephews, stood near us. He wasn't famous. He didn't die young. And yet the people came, and came, a sweeping swell of every age whose lives he had touched in some way.

If one were to look at a photomontage of Irish ancestry you would find a face and rakish appeal like Uncle Raymond's. His nose was large, his eyes were hazel with an upward slant, a trait common to the Burn's family. A strong physique and ruddy complexion testified to his many years in the out of doors. He wore an Irish cap or wool fedora in the winter and a Panama hat in the summer. Penny loafers without socks, an Irish knit sweater, and green corduroy pants completed his usual ensemble. He had a spring to his step and a gentle laugh that came easily, a hearty "hello" to the many who waved to say just "Ray" as he was out and about.

Raymond's love of the "black earth" and the tenderness that he showed to nature was a reflection of the way he conducted his life. The gardens of the estates in Newport were his extended family of love, and he spent many hours planting and pruning the flowerbeds until well into his eighth decade. He relished showing off those inner sanctums behind the high stone walls. A hush enveloped these grounds, and one sensed the need to speak softly lest the perfect order was disturbed. There was always a "Hi, Ray" from the groundskeeper, as we strolled the manicured pathways, as he pointed out the giant camellias, the various species of roses, gardenias, beds of petunias and impatience frolicking in the sun.

There were many facets to Raymond. He left a litany of good will that transcended the daily routine of life, for he shared all of his gifts, his love of history, his love of family, his love of music, his love of nature. Golf was his sport and he played at the Wanumetonomy Golf Club. There was always a golf tournament in the summer and once his brother, Uncle Charlie, got a hole in one that was thoroughly celebrated with a pint or two.

Perhaps his greatest gift was his ability to make you feel special for he seemed to discern a person's uniqueness. Welcomed wherever he went, he'd drop by Barbara's for a swim in her pool, or celebrate St. Patrick's Day at Maureen's, or take a run out to little Charlie's to see his grandniece and nephew. He made it a point to spend time with the "kids" who did not live in Newport, journeys that took him to my home every Thanksgiving, or to see Jackie Burns in Florida, or his great nephew Michael Lynch in Washington. He would take the Ferry from New London to visit my brother who lives in Long Island, and as the great nieces and nephews increased, he kept in touch with all of them, a daunting task, but one he accomplished with ease, for that was Raymond.

My cousins Barbara and Kim took him to Ireland for it had

been many years since he had walked on the old sod and visited our Irish cousins. He often told the story of his first trip to Ireland when he was a young man, how his heart swelled when he stepped into that small thatched cottage in Ballygar and saw the beautiful face of his mother's sister, quietly sitting by the hearth.

Always thoughtful, he dropped off pumpkins on the doorsteps of his nieces and nephews every Halloween, and at Christmas a beautiful poinsettia would arrive at my home. In the spring and summer he cut a bouquet from his garden to give to whomever he visited. I can see him now, dressed and ready. "Just a sec, Patsy, I want to clip a few roses, and those dahlia's are looking good, too." A quick foray into the flowers and then we would be off.

He was always deferential to women, tipping his cap or his straw hat, a perfect gentleman, so it is no wonder that a wealthy widow whose gardens he maintained took a shine to him and invited him to tea. Well, he was a wreck, but he got all shined and polished and went and had a lovely time, even though he took some ribbing from the crew.

Ray was a wonderful dancer and at social gatherings he was always in demand. He made it a point to have a "spin" with all the girls, and unescorted "ladies." He loved to dance to "New York, New York" and when that downbeat began his eyes would light up and someone would always say, "C'mon Ray." His response. "Great, kid, great."

If something bothered him he'd shake his head and say, "Damn shame." But, he usually took great joy in those around him. Every evening he enjoyed a "taste" and fixed himself a Manhattan that he'd sip slowly as he read the paper and did the crossword puzzle. Raymond was the historian of the Ancient Order of Hibernians and on Wednesday evening's he would walk over to the Hibernian Hall on Wellington Avenue to meet his friend Pat Murphy who shared a love of Irish history.

As the years passed and I grew from a child into an adult we still took quiet walks through the gardens or a spin around the Ocean Drive. When he visited we always had an adventure and he would laugh his easy laugh and call me a "homing pigeon" as I negotiated the highways to West Point, Hyde Park, Bear Mountain, or Jockey Hollow and the Golf Museum in Morristown, NJ. He arranged to have my grandparent's names on the immigrant wall at Ellis Island and on a spring day one

May, he and I, and my second cousin, Nancy Meehan, took the boat from Liberty State Park. Always sentimental, when we found their names his eyes filled with tears, perhaps for their long journey and his long life.

He was a huge presence in my life, a man who listened, and a man who always seemed to speak of interesting things. And yet, he conveyed the impression that the person he was speaking with was imbued with marvelous qualities like intelligence, kindness, empathy and good will. Raymond lived to the age of eighty-nine, sowing good deeds and kindness and beauty like the flowers he loved.

### ❦

# *Aunt Elaine*

She was special, my Aunt Elaine. We gravitated toward each other, probably because I was a kid and she acted like one. Elaine was my Uncle Joe's wife, and though she wasn't the family's favorite, she was mine. She was only thirteen years older than me. She was different, which in my family means she wasn't Italian, and my grandmother had no tolerance for anyone who would dare marry a child of hers who wasn't Italian. Aunt Elaine's parents were Christian Science people of English descent. She was also six feet plus to Uncle Joe's five foot three. When they married, pictures were taken at a park; she sitting on a bench and Uncle Joe standing next to her. They were the same height! Nonny always said he married her because he felt sorry for her, she was so big and her family so poor. From what Aunt Elaine told me later on, she reached six foot in grade school and she *didn't* have a happy childhood; quite the opposite. What Nonny neglected to remember was the fact that Uncle Joe was born without his left hand, which certainly didn't attract many young women. The couple stayed together in spite of my grandmother's feelings. When Elaine's mom passed away, her father had one girlfriend after another. They all made fun of her height and weight; one of them even put a lock on the icebox. Sad for a young girl who was unhappy to begin with.

Anyway, this little Rita was happy he married her. Aunt Elaine

saved me from being the butt of my brothers' teasing. Each weekend
that I didn't have to go to my grandmother's to practice piano lessons she
would swoop over to our house and whisk me away. We did things my
mother would never do with me. Mom was upset because I *loved* going
for the weekend whenever I could. I would get so excited when I knew
Aunt Elaine was coming. I secretly had a bag with a change of clothes
under my bed for these occasions, so no time would be wasted before my
leaving.

Aunt Elaine loved celebrities and all music. She would take
me to the Mosque theatre in Newark where we saw and listened to
operettas, operas sung in English, and I'm sure it's where I learned to love
the opera. I even saw Lionel Hampton and his xylophone at the Avon
Theatre; a real celebrity! I was thrilled!

Elaine loved Frank Sinatra, too. The room I slept in on those
weekends had a full length poster hanging on the door of the skinny little
kid with the big Adam's apple and silly bow tie. Considering Uncle Joe's
height, and Frank's, maybe she had a thing for short men.

My mother never seemed to care that I was gone from Friday
night to Sunday evening. It seemed that because she was angry that
I *so* looked forward to leaving, she didn't care if I ever came home. *I*
sure didn't! Being with Aunt Elaine was like having a sleep over with a
girlfriend. She talked to me like another girl would talk to a close friend.
I felt so loved with her. And Uncle Joe was my favorite uncle. I wished I
was their kid. I was about seven or maybe younger when this relationship
began, and we did this weekend thing until my family moved to the shore
when I was eleven.

My aunt used to draw pictures of families and tell a story about
them while she drew. We would sit at the kitchen table, and my eyes
would be glued to the paper, fascinated at how easily the stories came to
her. I wish I had kept some of them; they were so precious. We played
with paper dolls, and she would tell spooky stories at night when Uncle
Joe fell asleep. One story was so horrible, I still remember it! It was
about a dog so frightened by ghosts it turned itself inside out! It scared
the stuffing out of me! We'd giggle and eat junk food, wash and set each
other's hair; and go downtown to the hustle and bustle of working people,
smelling the smells of the peanut store, eat soft pretzels 'til we felt sick,

and just walk around, people watching. This big, tall, heavy woman with the short brown hair and beautiful green eyes was my very best friend.

Aunt Elaine had a chip on her shoulder as big as a boulder, though. When folks stared at her largeness she wasn't shy about staring right back, exclaiming loudly, "what the hell are you looking at?" This would intimidate the gawkers and they would look away. Sometimes I would be embarrassed for her, but deep down I was angry at people's hurtful remarks made as we passed by. Only I knew what a tender-hearted person she was; and the power she possessed. Among her many attributes, my Aunt Elaine was psychic; she was sensitive to extrasensory feelings. She never flaunted it or talked about it to everyone, but she did to me. I think I was *her* best friend during these times. Aunt Elaine found things for people. She would contact her spirit guide or whoever and minutes later would divulge the whereabouts of the lost object. It was really something to see! Her ability was used sparingly, and only for certain people. I think she was a little afraid of her own power. Aunt Elaine explained to me that her mother had this ability, too. I grew up with other family members with ESP and other phenomenon, so I wasn't frightened, just totally interested! For having this ability, she should have fit into my family; but still she was considered an outcast.

We both went from paper dolls to reality when Aunt Elaine lost the little girl she was carrying, the baby she waited so long for. She was so heavy that most of the family didn't even know she was pregnant! Some of the childishness was lost after that. I missed that part of her. It took a long while for it to come back. When it did return somewhat, Elaine and I resumed our travels by bus to downtown with an addition to our usual haunts; my grieving aunt would buy a bunch of daffodils from a vendor and we would detour to the cemetery. I would cry along with her as she sobbed and spoke to her lost little girl, Joyce Ann. Always a bunch of daffodils...

When we moved to the shore we two lost the closeness we had, but years later, happily, we connected again. After Tony and I married and the kids were a little older, she and Uncle Joe would come and spend weekends with us. It was a switch, and we both were happy to pick up where we left off years before. While Tony and Uncle Joe would bond (which meant sleeping in front of the television), Aunt Elaine and I became kids again. We went to the movies, walked the boards and the beach, ate salt water taffy, her favorite, and giggled at everything and nothing. It was a pleasant change from being a mother and wife, the sometimes boredom of married life. Aunt Elaine was my 'happy' fix.

Until she passed away, she was still one of my best friends. Aunt Elaine put the fun in my childhood. She always said we were sisters in another life. Even after she had a little girl years later, she always called me her first daughter. Being around my aunt was like being wrapped in a warm, loving blanket. When her daughter moved to New Mexico, I lost Elaine again. She moved to be near her daughter Dona, and her new twin grandchildren. Every time she saved enough money though, she would come up and stay with me. The ocean she loved was not to be found in Albuquerque, and we would be at the beach every day she was with us. Elaine always said she would like to come back as a whale; her weight would not raise eyebrows under the sea. Aunt Elaine died the evening before my 70th birthday and on the way to her granddaughter's wedding reception. The little girl in me died then, too. Dona sent me her ashes, and because she loved the ocean, my son and I scattered them off the jetty after a short ceremony. I'm sure that made my Aunt Elaine happy.

I have a special feeling for whales now.

# *what if*

would the grass be
greener
if I stared long enough

would the clouds go by
faster
if I watched carefully

would the sky be
bluer
if I could touch it

would the sea rise to
meet me
should I step in its path

would the world never
end
if I held on tight

would you love me
more
if I needed you to?

# A Letter To Raymond

Dear Raymond;

    I think I know what it's like to wake up from a tornado. That chilling silence after everything's been destroyed. Moving through your life, wondering what's left. Trying to figure out whether it's finally safe or did the devil simply spare you for future torment.

    Since you've been gone, we've had tornadoes every Friday. The storm comes and tears our lives apart; whatever portions still remain. Afterwards, we stumble through the debris and then realize – this is how we live.

    I don't know if we'll recover from this last one. It wasn't Mommy's typical Friday night twister. It was worse; debris was everywhere. I walked through the entire house Saturday morning, recalling the breaking of each glass and ashtray; the overturning of every chair. You should see the dinette table; it's now bowed in the middle from two collapsing legs. I can't remember who fell on it. Dinner from Friday night before was never put away; it's a shame too, it was the best lasagna I ever made.

    Mommy's friend Eddie was still asleep on the couch. He was fully stretched out, his shoes off and using his coat as a blanket. I kept wondering why he hadn't gone home, since he only lived three doors down.

Mommy was still asleep, too. Hard. The dead-like sleep she does when a pound of liquor beats her down. I peeked in her room to see her sprawled across the bed on top of the covers still wearing the clothes she had on yesterday. It was a turbulent day. Between hands of Bid Whist and shots of Johnny Walker Red, she managed to curse us all out. You know how card games go with Mommy. If she's sober, it's a fun filled family night. If she's drunk, we all pay the price. What always starts out as a few friendly games of cards, somehow ends up in Mommy's drunken 'blasts to the past'– serenaded by the moans of Al Green.

She sits and mouths these mellow songs and then takes huge sips from her jelly jar. Every song and sip seem to remind her of all the wrong her life has endured. She starts to reminisce. She told Eddie about every shameful moment our family ever had. The time Daddy's brother went to jail; the time you all drove to Brooklyn to stop that drug dealer from pimping our cousin Delores; and even the rumor that Daddy was having an affair with Miss Anna. You remember her. That wild hell of a humdinger that lived two doors down – back when we lived in the Projects. She was always after Daddy. Thought he was the money train out of Brooklyn! But that's OK, 'cause they both ain't no damn good! They deserve each other!

That's what Mommy says.

She was on a winning streak, that night. She and Vincent were partners. They won three games in a row. I had hoped that winning would keep her spirits up; you know, happy drunk. But the music made her melancholy with a side twist of indignation. The more she won, the more she kept snapping her cards on the table, as if to say, "how dare we play against her." After a while, everyone just wanted to go to bed.

She started berating everybody. Moving from one child to the next; calling out the error of our ways. You were far too outspoken and defied her until the day you left. And of course she mentioned Kevin getting Denise pregnant. She never said a word about Vincent, though. I think she loves him more because he's Vincenté's son. Remember how she used to say, "Vincenté left me to die in a war, but your father left me to sleep with my friends." We've paid a heavy price for being Carl's children.

146

I feel sorry for Andrew the most. He loves her so much more than the rest of us, yet she yells at him just the same. I left the room, before she even got to me – cause you know, when she gets to me all hell breaks loose! Everything about me unnerves her. My 21 year old breast on my age 12 body; my straight-A, "Miss-Priss" attitude that seems to scream out that I'm better than her. I headed straight upstairs, the moment she started the sentence, "you gotdamned kids. . ."

Kevin tried to change the subject. He told a story about the Cavanaugh's new dog. This little punk ass Chihuahua that always runs around trying to bite everybody's ankles. Sometimes you just wanted to stomp that dog or at least, accidentally run the car over it. Last month, Trinka nearly killed it. She had it pinned down and was about to take a huge chunk from it's throat before Vincent stopped her. Of course, we all momentarily wished he had let her do it.

Mommy listened to the story for a while, seeming to be amused. She didn't even realize she'd been drinking straight water. That's a new tactic I came up with; diluting her drinks. But the Trinka story didn't work. Mommy was only momentarily distracted by a small sense of pride. I guess she thought it was only right that God would at least give her a kick-ass dog, given the rest of her life was so shitty. She told Eddie how she had personally picked Trinka from the litter. She knew a good dog when she saw one; even if it was a female.

Yea, right!

But things got worse, after Vincent opened his stupid mouth. He brought up that story about you and him skating in the hallway. You remember that time the two of you were taking laps around the elevator shaft? Racing, round and round, until you ran smack dead into the wall and busted your lip wide open. Blood was shooting everywhere. Mommy was down in Aunt Sue's apartment so he ran and got *Miss Anna.* And that was the one name we didn't need to hear that night; Miss Anna!

Vincent and Andrew were busy cracking up about the story, but I could see the storm brewing inside Mommy. You all liked Miss Anna so much, but Mommy hated her guts. Andrew thought she was so pretty. Remember, how he used to sit on her lap and she'd whisper in his ear? When he was little, he used to pretend one of my dolls was Miss Anna and give it kisses. Mommy made him stop. Told him, "Miss Anna ain't no damn doll!" She sure must've put some kind of "Mo-Jo" on that boy. That's why he's so weak for light-skinned girls now; cause Miss Anna done something to him. She tried the same thing on all you boys.

That's what Mommy says.

From upstairs, I could hear the yelling and the chairs moving around the floor. That meant the game was officially over. Mommy was stomping her foot and yelling at the same time. She has this new move, where she puts her hand on her hip and pounds her foot into the ground. With each stomp, she'll yell out her curse words. Shit – Got – damn – it!

Then, she started telling Eddie about the time she found Daddy. I guess it was because Miss Anna's name came up. You know that story all too well. Mommy's single moment of strategic brilliance, when she dragged us along on her early morning pilgrimage to Brooklyn; still in our ragged pajamas. Knocking, door to door on every apartment; screaming at the inhabitants, "is this where Carl Stewart lives?"

I remember Kevin and I being particularly mortified by the whites who answered. They'd stare at our worn t-shirts and oversized long-johns, stained and holey. You could see the confusion and pity in their eyes. Those – *should I call child services?*' – eyes. Those – *'what kind of woman is this?*' – eyes. Mommy looked crazy, moving boldly through their building. The five of us; holding hands in chain link. She hadn't bothered to comb her hair or change clothes from the day before. Her dress was wrinkled from half a night's sleep. It was torn under the arm and had a permanent grease stain.

She knocked on all the doors of the first and second floor. One old lady threatened to call the cops. Mommy simply dared her. Apartment 3H turned out to be the ticket. A young light skinned girl with long brown hair answered. She reminded me of Miss Anna, but it wasn't her. A daughter or sister, perhaps. Mommy screamed at her and leaped into the apartment. The girl tried to make us stay in the hallway, but Mommy pushed her against the door and dragged Vincent by his shirt. He was lead hand holder and so we were all forced to follow.

Daddy finally came out of a back room. I could tell he just woke up, still in his t-shirt and underwear. His first words were, "what the hell is going on…?" A sentence he need not finish. We were standing right there in his apartment.

I kept wondering why you couldn't do anything about this. You were only eleven back then, but you had always been able to rescue us from Mommy's full scale rages. You got us back inside, when she locked us out; got her to open up the bathroom door, when she threatened suicide. You even got us dinner, when she refused to cook. But I guess this was way over your head.

Daddy told Mommy to keep it down, while he went back to get some pants. She kept cursing and calling him names. The young girl tied up her robe. It was clear, she'd been sleeping on the couch. She started folding up blankets and picking up clothes off the living room floor.

Mommy was yelling, louder and louder. She kept yanking Vincent's hand, causing the rest of us to jerk and wobble. She screamed at Daddy to come back. It was so loud, it actually hurt my ears. Like a fool, I let a *sob* come out. Kevin yanked my hand to tell me to stop, but it was too late. The pity of it all had started to wear on me. He and Andrew were squeezing my hands so tight, they were numb. I desperately had to go to the bathroom and when I looked down, I realized I had cut my foot. I didn't really know how bad it was, until I turned and saw my footprints in blood. They followed me from the door. I cried harder.

Daddy pulled Mommy aside and they started to argue. I couldn't hear everything but I knew it was about money. He shook his head and started heading towards the door, but then Mommy yelled out, "where is she? I just want to see her. Come on out, Anna!" She turned towards the young girl and shouted, "Who's this? You and Anna making babies now?"

"That's my brother's daughter, Sandy, and you know it! Just cut the crap! I'll take you down to the deli and cash a check. And then you can get your ass out of here!"

We were still standing near the doorway. Vincent moved us slightly to the side, but I could only drag my foot. It was in pain. The blood puddle was bigger. Daddy pushed Mommy through the door, while he shoved his feet into some sandals. He grabbed his keys from a small table and motioned us to stay. Mommy quickly grabbed Vincent and pulled him with her. The door swung closed.

The rest of us stood motionless. We didn't know what to do. We didn't know our cousin's name. She didn't know ours'. She kept cleaning for a while, but eventually noticed the large red spots on the floor and traced them to me. Her eyes offered pity, so I gave her my hand. She cleaned me in the bathroom and put a pair of socks on my feet. The cut was bad. It bled through the band-aid and the sock, but at least, it didn't puddle.

Daddy came back an hour later, without Mommy and Vincent. His niece kept telling us to sit down, but we just stood there. Daddy kept looking at us and shaking his head. He kept repeating his favorite saying: "oh, my aching back!"

We stayed until the sun rose and set. Daddy fixed us chili and we ate. Mommy and Vincent came back to get us, at ten. I was asleep.

\* \* \*

By the time she was done with her story, Eddie and Vincent were slapping Mommy high-fives. I never understood why Vincent was so proud of that story. The rest of us still carry the shame. After she was done, she poured another drink and gulped it down. No ice. The heat must've risen to her head and made her dizzy. She stumbled into the counter and nearly dropped her jar, but she caught it against her body.

I was hiding behind the staircase. I motioned Andrew to come upstairs before it got worse. He moved from the couch and tried to quietly pass them at the table, but the movement drew her attention. She started yelling that she needed us gone. She couldn't take it anymore and Daddy had gotten off scot-free for years. "Pack your stuff," she yelled. "I want all of you out in the morning!" Mommy looked around and caught sight of me and Andrew at the stairwell. "I told you damn kids to pack your stuff!" Andrew jumped from his crouched position. He cried out but Mommy screamed right back at him, "did you hear me?"

In one motion, she pushed Vincent to the side and threw her jar against the table. It exploded! Thick pieces of glass flew everywhere. Vincent slipped against the table trying to avoid the pieces, but Kevin spun around and grabbed his right eye. He was hit. Blood was gushing from his face. He screamed at her, but she didn't seem to care.

"Dammit, Mommy!" Vincent examined Kevin's eye and said

150

they'd have to go to the hospital. It needed stitches. He put a dish cloth against Kevin's face and walked him through the door.

I couldn't believe how indifferent she was. She just calmly headed to her bedroom and reminded me and Andrew to pack our stuff. Eddie just sat there on the couch. We never heard Vincent and Kevin come back. Andrew and I fell asleep exhausted from crying; exhausted from fear.

Saturday morning I was cleaning up the broken glass when Vincent and Kevin finally walked through the door. They spent the entire night at the emergency room. We all spoke softly trying not to awaken Mommy. I wanted badly to clean up before she woke. I thought, if I could remove the remnants of last night, she would simply forget. We used the broom on the carpet to sweep up. The vacuum cleaner made far too much noise. Andrew used Pledge on all the tables. The room smelled fresh.

Eddie finally woke up and Mommy soon after. We tried to avoid eye contact with her – moving and cleaning. "No need to clean that up," she said. "Just go pack your stuff. I'm taking you over to your father's. Be ready in an hour"

The soul drained from my body, like an open sink. This was it. Mommy kept her voice low and steady. I thought about crying and telling her I didn't want to go. I thought about working my plea into a frenzy and then collapsing to the floor. Eventually, in the midst of tears and shivers, I would promise that we'd be more obedient and studious and less troublesome. Not that I knew exactly what we'd done wrong. But then, I decided *not* to cry.

I saw Andrew lean the broom against the wall. His eyes welled. He glanced at me, waiting to see what I would do. I knew he was prepared to plead, but I wasn't. My duffle bag was packed within the hour.

I wanted to call you then and there, but Kevin said not to. He said that your college days should be peaceful; that school gave you enough to worry about. He warned me not to tell you what was going on. He went to stay with Glenn Mashburn. Mommy told him to make sure he had permanent arrangements.

But Vincent didn't have to leave. Mommy let him stay. In fact, he drove us all the way to Brooklyn. He and Mommy talked about fishing and re-tiling the bathroom floor. They planned their week. Andrew and I sat in the back, numb. Our stomachs, empty.

Daddy was waiting in front of his building. He grabbed our bags and headed straight upstairs. Mommy didn't say good-bye. Vincent never got out of the car. I knew then, I hated him.

We've been here at Daddy's for 3 weeks. Andrew has insisted we call every day begging Mommy to let us come home. Vincent answers the phone like we're gotdamned strangers. One time, he said, "Mommy's not here, but I'll let her know that you called."

I can't wait for that son-of-a-bitch to die.

Last weekend, Daddy took us to see his brother. Guess what? He lives just outside of Boston, less than an hour away from your school. I asked Daddy if we could drive up to see you, but he never answered me. And I saw our cousin, you know, the pretty one who visited Daddy. Her name is Clarice. She's still nice.

This morning, I told Andrew if he wanted to go home he'd have to do his own begging. I'm not asking anymore. He even said I should ask you to call Mommy; because you're always able to pull us out. You know, like when we were kids. But that's not why I'm writing. I just wanted to send you our new address; care of Carl Stewart.

I miss you.

Love always,
Your only sister

P.S. I think I know what it's like to wake up from a tornado. That chilling silence after everything's been destroyed. Moving through your life, wondering what's left. Trying to figure out whether it's finally safe, or did the devil simply spare you for future torment. And after the storm, you stumble through the debris and finally realize – you have to start all over.

# *Drowning*

like gasping
for that last mouthful of air –
as though she could still manage to save her own life –

it was hopeless,
cause she'd made up her mind –
or maybe,
Johnny Walker made it up for her.

trapped in a fog,
somewhere between Valium and eighty proof –
this,
her last straw.

unable
to articulate what triggered it –
unnerved
that they required a reason –

being tortured,
by a moment in time she
should've said, no – to the ghosts and dead saints,

whispering the same things,
over and over,
until she hastens
to a four-walled corner – glaring down her last second of clarity.

# *Heredity*

She said,
I carried myself
like street trash, like
a girl
never properly raised.
A girl who settled
for pennies
and dimes and gave her spirit
away for
free.
She said,
her love could
never be bountiful
because
I was too much like
him –
a man who journeyed
from house to home,
but never
took in the view.
Once,
when she was saying
her words to me,
words my body
could now
repeat–
I discovered the
source of my wilding –
it was rooted beneath her dress.
she was standing
over me, pounding her foot,
swaying her hips,
beating her curse
into the wind.
she raised her arms
to swing at me
alas, I saw her skin.
it was black.
it was blue.

# Mementos

# *Merely a Girl*

My mother sat in the new black dress, the age-old costume of death, weary and dry-eyed. She was thin almost to the point of anorexia. Only her hands gave away any sign of emotion. The twisted, arthritic, wrinkled hands grasped each other until the knuckles turned white. The motion had to be painful, but not a flicker of pain showed on her face. She was worn out from crying, from greeting people who had known her husband. Even more so, from caring for my father the past few years. *How did you carry on when in his pain he grew cranky and mean?* But I knew she loved him dearly, her heart was always his. She cared for him without complaint, though she had to stop working to stay home with him the last few years.

The funeral parlor was cold, and the smell of flowers consumed the room. My throat closed with the cloying scent. *When I die I don't want one damned flower in the room. I hate lilies especially, with their large white, unemotional petals, and I hate whoever decreed that they should be death's chosen bloom.*

*I miss you already, Daddy. It wasn't my Catholic mother who took me to church on Sundays- it was you, my Jewish father, who promised to raise any offspring Catholic if the church allowed him to marry mom. You kept your promise.*

*Though it was unusual to nurture girls in this family-boys were the*

159

*ruling class- you broke the rule with me.* It was only the women, though, who didn't value girls; my mother, her sister, her grandmother. My brothers were often given gifts and new clothes, but none for me. I was nine when my Nonny told me she had little use for girls. So I shouldn't have been surprised by my mother's attitude. She always seemed formidable to me as a child. To this day I don't remember getting a hug, a kiss or a kind word. The permanent frown on her face seemed forever centered on me.

"Why do you tell people that Tommy and Junior are so good and helpful to you, and I'm useless?" I asked plaintively, hating the whine in my voice. *I* had to do the same chores they did, but she always praised them for doing theirs. Mom said girls were worthless. Why couldn't I just ask, "what did I ever do to make you not like me?" But I knew what the answer would be: "I never favored the boys over you- it's all in your mind." Her smiles were only for them, and though my school marks far exceeded theirs, they were praised for their C's. If they got into trouble, it was fondly said of them, "Typical boys!" But Dad was proud of me, and he let me know it. His love was my saving grace, and I embraced it gratefully.

Now he lay in the silver coffin. Though I've heard the expression, "Doesn't he look good?" of the dead, Daddy really did. The soft pink lighting above the casket softened his swarthy face, making him look relaxed and serene. The face didn't show the pain or stress on the over-medicated body that had been my father's since illness overtook him.

Towards the end of the evening the crowd had thinned out, leaving the immediate family the finality of saying goodbye to the beloved husband, father, grandfather, lying there at the front of the room. Something pulled me toward the coffin. Was he calling me to say goodbye? It felt that way. *I'm coming, Dad.* I rose from the mourning chair, his essence beckoning to me. I knelt before him, and memories flowed over me in waves. This was my last time with my father, this man I loved dearly. Everyone in the room faded away; it was just him and me.

*"Remember when you took me to the circus, Daddy? You let me reach out and touch the elephants. I still remember the feel of their coarse, hairy bodies; I never knew elephants had hair! I don't know where the boys were on this trip to the big top; I didn't care- I had you all to myself! And how I loved going*

*deep-sea fishing with you, especially because Tommy and Junior got seasick and couldn't go with us. Was it bad that I was happy it was just me and you? Except for that time you let me bring Theresa and she got so sick you said, "no more girlfriends." And remember the first time I got a nibble and got so excited, I let go of your fishing pole and lost it to the deep blue sea? You never said a word, just overlooked my humiliation with a hug. Do you recall the huge fight you and Mom had one night, so loud it woke me, and in her anger she asked me who I would rather be with? Well, it was no surprise I chose the one who loved and valued me. So she threw us both out! Tommy and Junior woke up, but mommy's little pets wanted to stay in bed. "What am I going to do with you, Kiddo?" Then you took me to work the next morning in the big red UCO truck you drove. I got to take the day off from school! The best words I ever heard were when you told me you always wanted a little girl after having just boys. You made me feel so special."*

A light tap on my shoulder halted my last moments with my father.

"Rita, it's nine o'clock, they're closing up; we have to leave." My mother on one side and my husband on the other gently but forcefully lifted me away from my final private moments with my dad. I kissed his cold cheek and I could have sworn the small curve on his lips hadn't been there before.

Only a few years later Mom passed away; too late for confrontations or apologies. Maybe had I told her even once that I loved her; maybe that would have made a difference. Probably not...I simply wasn't a boy.

# Island Storms

I know the time and distance
between each star in the sky.
I've counted and measured them,
waiting for the words to arrive.
Fluttered sounds and empty meanings –
when no one's left to hear.

sands that race through my fingers,
leaving behind a lonely grain –
mocking what's left of my life.

The tornados took everyone away –
a wild wind that hurled them across the sea.
Tearing apart the lies we had built.  Our stories,
now without binding or cover.

She said she was glad they were gone.
It was their fault the storms had come.
they had brought the rage –
to an otherwise contented life.

if not for them, she would've been young.
her talents could've taken her away.
but instead,  she withered –
caring for their starving souls.

And now I was left alone, with her.
Left to sort the bones and parts
her love refused to save.

She sat staring at a colorless sky,
feeling nothing of the world around her.
I knew she was recording her past. Lives,
she had been entitled to,  but never received.

I walked around her, softly,
not even parting the air, as I passed.
I too, should've been taken with the storms.
She said she wanted all of us gone,
yet she held my feet when the winds came.

not out of love, but misery.
To force me to be with her,
to hear her cries. To curse me,
when the tides washed away her castles.

when the others were here, she did not see me.
It was her eyes that failed. For
I could cry and not be heard.

I liked it that way.
measuring the stars had become my pastime.
and when words would not come, I could
blame the stars and their distance.

but now we're alone, she and I.
no words to speak, no parts to love
and all our mediators are gone.

# *Driftwood*

He called it a family heirloom; as if their family owned anything worth passing on. This driftwood coffee table. A water-weathered, twisted, interlocking branch painted and stressed in antique white. It had naturally sculptured arms of wood with raw edges and knotted sides. Tiny veins of gold paint accented the finish. A vine of plastic red flowers was weaved and twined through the knots, robbing the wood of its rustic elegance. A statement of sensual art; sawed and leveled with a glass top…

It had a matching floor lamp with a bright red shade!

\* \* \*

It took their mother, Sandy, eight months to pay it off; – on lay-away. She spotted it one winter evening displayed in Stevenson's window, flanked by sage green tufted couches and a flowered club chair. Sandy thought it her dream table; so different, so crude, it was classy – just because.

She kept her eight month investment a secret. Squeezing out a $5 dollar weekly payment from an already strained budget. But it was her one self-gift. A chance to have something *nice,* for once in her life.

She left work early, the evening it was delivered; forgoing her weekend fifth of scotch to make that final lump payment of $15.20. Her smile gleaming and bursting, as they set the table in front of the couch.

165

Her five children stood dazzled by their first piece of fine furniture recognizing that its odd look meant class.

Sandy divvied out her care instructions. Celia was to clean it every day; no water; just Windex on the top. No glasses or bottles without coasters. Raymond and Kevin were to rotate it weekly, so the bottom wouldn't permanently indent the carpet. And she warned Andrew, no more running in the living room. Someone could fall and break the glass top.

Sandy began her quest for the matching lamp immediately. Seven dollars a week.

The table became a centerpiece of conversation. Visitors admired this rare sense of style, uncommon to black folk. But over the years, Celia had developed a more intriguing story of its acquisition. She told one friend that her father brought it in Korea; that he often brought home odd pieces and trinkets from his trips abroad. He was a navy man; always at sea – thus explaining why he was never around...

Only the last part was true. He *was* a navy man.

\* \* \*

When Sandy died, Celia was the only one with enough room in her home to take the table and lamp. They never asked if she wanted it. It was merely assumed. After all, it was an heirloom and someone would have to care for it.

The pieces had indeed weathered over the years. The glass top was broken leaving a dangerous rough edge in the front. Most of the flowers were gone and the gold vein had faded. The lamp no longer worked and the bright red shade was torn and ragged. The care instructions had certainly been ignored in later years.

Kevin stared at Celia as though she'd just won the lottery. *You lucky – stiff.* She'd get to take home Sandra's most prized possession. Did she know the value or respect its memory?

Though her home was indeed eclectic, she couldn't figure out how to merge the pieces. Celia's style was early American with an African flare; hand carved wooden masks over the Queen Anne chair. The red, purple and gold Indonesian Temple Window over the fireplace mantle didn't seem to match. The bust of King Tutankhamen, rescued from the trash of a Broadway set; sitting on the faux marble pedestal. Celia's style was a medley of senses.

The glass top was carefully discarded. The antique paint was power washed clean. The carpenter had leveled the lamp so that it too could lay flush and level on the floor. Solid wood planks, beveled and carved in a kidney shape mimicked the pool's edge. The new wooden benches around Celia's pool became a centerpiece of conversation. Rustic and artistic. Compelling even her wealthiest neighbors to wonder which of the posh, exclusive, country stores had made the custom piece.

And the Korean stories were now gone; no more tales of naval seaport adventures. Celia simply described the pride and joy of a working mother; buying herself one small slice of elegance.

## *Brown Haired Girl*

I have mementos of Mom's that are tucked away, some forgotten, others displayed or used like the crystal wine glasses, the exquisite cameo that belonged to my Nana, her pearls, a favorite gold and gem studded charm I wear on a chain around my neck. The photo albums, cards and notes to the children or me are packed in boxes in the attic. One day when I was up there looking for something I came across a small carton, with its contents neatly wrapped in newspaper. As I unfolded the first piece I recognized my mother's Art Deco vanity set, a collection in vivid orange with sharp black trim. There is a brush, a mirror, two small boxes with glass containers for creams, an oblong receptacle, and a rectangular box. A nail file with a fancy handle and a nail buffer in a case complete this unusual ensemble of dresser wares. The jars and nail accouterments and miscellaneous boxes are reminiscent of a time when ladies sat before their vanities in silk robes applying Pond's Cold Cream to their faces.

I do not know how it came to my mother. It seems to me the flashy presence of the set did not suit her, for her strength and compassion simmered with a firm, gentle light. And yet there was a time when the reed thin young woman with jet black hair and hazel eyes left her home in Newport, RI to study nursing in New York. There was a time when she lived in Greenwich Village on Christopher Street when speakeasies and jazz and raccoon coats were the rage. Perhaps it was a token from a grateful patient for Mom was a gifted nurse and often had well-to-do people in her care. Perhaps it was a wedding gift from a stylish friend who selected it in an art boutique in the village.

My childhood memories cannot find the secret to this set, yet I know Mom displayed it for a while, then kept it safe, perhaps out of the way of children's sticky hands.

As I unwrap the paper and open the containers I find a lock of my childhood hair tied in a pink ribbon. It is chestnut brown with auburn highlights, slightly curled at the end. A small piece of paper in her handwriting says, "Patsy's hair, 1940." I was two years old. As I gently remove it from the box a kaleidoscope of emotions color the moment. I see her gently place the lock of hair in the bright orange box and close the lid, my baby hair safe in its orange glow waiting to be found.

When I hold the hair in my hand it is slightly dry, but still silky and soft, and imparts a feeling of sweet sadness for that child of so long ago, and the young woman with the lustrous long brown hair. And I think that maybe this lock of hair is a metaphor for life, its growth and vibrancy often shorn, its color changed like jobs or lovers, its style in touch with the times or kept in the same unflinching bob, swaying to its own persona.

I think that our hair is a benchmark for events in our lives. Our wedding, the depleted strands after giving birth, the ghastly puffed up lacquered helmet that set off the bridesmaid's dress from hell, the first silver streaks. Oh, we laugh and groan at the pictures in the family album and think, "Oh, my God, look at that hair!"

I think of the girl with the long brown hair who walked into a salon in Rome, Italy across from the Spanish Steps and left shorn in an Audrey Hepburn pixie. It is still cut in a short, breezy style, but now it is white, and I am my mother, gathering pieces of life like scattered ribbons in the breeze. I wrap my hair in the same-yellowed paper and return it to the glossy orange box, safe in its cocoon of the past. It is said that hair continues to grow after you're dead. Maybe then.

# *Midnight in Paris*

The dark blue bottle sat on the bureau in its place of prominence. It was my mother's favorite perfume, Midnight in Paris. A short, squat, round-shouldered bottle, it didn't look impressive. But it was the only perfume my mother ever wore. She used it sparingly, for there wasn't much money in our household, and perfume was definitely a luxury. My father bought her the last bottle quite some time ago; that was how miserly Mom was with it.

You could practically see the change in her attitude when she dabbed a little bit behind each ear; her whole personality shifted to happy. It made her smile, and my mother didn't smile much. Mom kept the bottle tightly closed, so as not to let the perfume evaporate or lessen its strength. She even kept the box, which was the same deep blue color as the bottle, and the inside was lined with a velvety soft material of the same color. The lettering on the box was done in silver, as was the Paris skyline. But mom never put the little bottle in the box; I think she liked looking at it.

Many years later I looked for the perfume for her. I thought it might make her smile again. She had been through a lot; she had lost her mother, her oldest son, and my father all in just a few years. Now she was nursing my other brother through chemotherapy and radiation. I couldn't find it anywhere, though.

When my mother passed away, I was going through her personal things. I opened her night table drawer, and there sat a dark blue, squat, round-shouldered, dusty bottle of Midnight in Paris. It was empty, but when I pulled the stopper I imagined that I could smell the familiar scent. And in my mind's eye I saw her smile when I dabbed the imaginary perfume behind each ear.

## *The Kiss*

The little girl sat on her mother's lap, and the two of them watched the snow floating down slowly, then quickly.  It became harder to see between the flakes.  Soon the land was covered in a thick white blanket.  Only the cool brightness from a winter moon reflecting off the snow gave light to the window where they sat in wonder at what was happening in the world outside.  The child was ecstatic that her mom let her stay up to see this, for it was way past her bedtime.  She clapped her little hands excitedly, leaning in to kiss her mother for offering this treat. Her mom hugged the small body tightly to her own in response.

The child was so enthralled with the winter scene, she hardly noticed that the woman on whose lap she sat was not smiling, but looked forlornly through the window.  The black and white picture out there pressed heavily against her heart.  How could the child, this little innocent, know that this evening was a special one? She had no knowledge of another little girl, who would have been her sister, whose birthday it would have been today.  And the kiss her mother gave back to her was really meant for the child buried somewhere out there beneath a mound of snow.

# *White Night*

It begins in the dead
     of night
A snowfall, deep and white

Its pearly, fragile flakes
Lose shape and melt away

The daylight brings a blinding
     mound
Of pristine shimmering ice

Sadly life takes over
The purity is gone

# Jobs

# *Lady Rachel*

I slipped into the black and white jersey Wilroy dress, a little swirl of positive and negative all the rage in the mid-sixties, added some bangle bracelets, and black straw low heeled pointy toe pumps. It was early Monday morning at the Jersey shore and another weekend of beach and bars was done. Time to rev up my blue Corvair (unsafe at any speed) and head up the Turnpike defying the semis, radio blasting, breeze in my hair. If I listen closely I can still hear the steady beat of "Summer in The City" pushing me forward to my job at ABC News.

The third network as it was then called was in high competitive gear with CBS and NBC and the documentary unit where I worked was a free wheeling cacophony of eccentric artistic types pushing hard. I was the Administrative Assistant, the only woman in an office with an eclectic assortment of writers, producers, directors and editors. I loved those guys, and in their own oddball ways they loved me back. Where else could a girl get a martini delivered in a paper cup at lunch when she was too busy to go out? When Ernie, a combination of Hercule Poirot and Groucho Marx sidled up to me, twisted his mustache and gleamed "…and how's my luscious little rosebud today, harrumph, harrumph," I was never offended, just bemused. One of the producers, Stuart, had narcolepsy and he'd fall asleep in the middle of a meeting. Just nod off. Sometimes he'd curl up in a corner on the floor and business went on as usual. Gordon, a sensitive, insecure kind of guy, was shooting a documentary about Timothy Leary and had hours and hours of film featuring a group of people strung out on LSD, rolling around on mats and pointing to Nirvana or whatever. The highlight of this footage was the dog, a German Shepherd on speed. Walter and Paulie, two of the editors were usually hung over and huddled over the movieola editing film, hot black coffee in hand.

We smoked, we drank, we produced a weekly television show on the Vietnam War, ABC Scope. Not the mouthwash. It was a prescient move, before the rage against the conflict took to the streets. Each week it was touch and go as to whether we'd get on the air because we had film shipped from Vietnam. Several couriers made the run between 67th Street and the airports. They were tough, like Hell's Angels, Harley's roaring into the cargo bay, large mesh bags filled with cans of film, film to be screened and edited. They hung out in the open office, big black buckled boots up on a desk, black leather jackets over their tattoos. Their leader was named Turk. We'd get the call, and off they would race, beating the plane as it made its descent into JFK or LaGuardia.

When the first big blackout hit New York in 1964 we were on high alert. We were dark, no news going out, but we worked all night in TV 1, the big studio, cranking out a show for when the lights came on. In the dark, with just candlelight, crews readied cable, anchors wrote stories and I put the scripts together. We got on the air at 7:00 a.m., cheering at our accomplishment. It was a great place to be.

Into this mix arrives Lady Rachel. My boss, Executive Producer and head of the documentary unit told me there was a girl coming in from London whose father was a big shot at the BBC and he wanted me to "take her under my wing." She blew in like a swallow caught in a wind tunnel, disheveled and unfocused. Her long brown hair flew like electric static, framing green eyes and a sharp pointed nose. And wouldn't you know she had that fine English skin. Unlike me in my sweet black and white she wore high suede boots in the mod fashion, the color of amber. Gorgeous and way out of my price range. She had some kind of a brocade vest over a wrinkled mini skirt and carried a carpetbag that kept spilling out scraps of paper, a lipstick, a tissue, a notebook when she dug into it. She had a run in her pantyhose and nothing seemed to match those elegant boots. But she was a Lady of the British Crown, a member of royalty on a mission to New York to learn the news business.

I was a QIC (Queens Irish Catholic) who came to work on the subway and went to college at night. And although I could help get a show on the air by candlelight I was no match for Lady Rachel for she was elusive as quicksilver. I took her to lunch at the Des Artiste's and showed her the workings of TV I, where the local and network news was aired. I introduced her to anyone who breathed and explained how our documentary unit functioned and her green-eyed attention wandered, the amber boots tapping. The thing was Lady Rachel had her own schedule, her own routine. She was a tempest in a teapot and I was way out of her league. She'd ta ta off in the middle of the day, "tea at the Plaza." She'd show up whenever she pleased, usually with some nifty preppy guy waiting in the wings. At the time I was dating a guy from the NYPD and he'd swing by in his squad car at lunch to say "hi." He was a movie star, tall, handsome, blue eyes, black hair. She spotted him, all right. "Who is that gorgeous man you were talking to?" Nothing like an Irish cop to get the blue blood boiling.

I guess she was used to servants because one evening she asked me to sew up a seam on a borrowed gown she was wearing to some fancy ball. There I am, fielding phone calls, typing script changes, dashing to the screening room, tripping over Stuart. A door across the room opens a crack and Rachel peeks out, "Patsy, Patsy," she calls. She's in a state of dishabille, in her bra, a gold satin gown halfway over her hips. The seam has ripped. She says, "I'm due at the Waldorf in a half hour and this damn gown ripped. Can you help me?" The "damn" gown was way too tight. We struggle getting it over her boobs. Then I staple her into the gown. I'm thinking it must be nice to be so free and sure of oneself to go to a ball in a stapled gown.

Nevertheless, Lady Rachel was handed a research assignment, a task that was the only way a girl could move ahead in the news business. I don't know if she ever did anything other than scatter papers around her carpetbag, but it was a bitter lesson for me and a taste of the power elite.

My goal was to move out of the "helper" role into a research or associate producer job. Ha, that was a big trick in 1965. There was one-woman associate producer at the network, Anne Morrissey. She was a firebrand, all of five foot two, with a freckled Irish face. There she'd be, army helmet on her head, knee deep in some trench in Vietnam. "This is Anne Morrissey reporting from Phon Nem" or whatever. She was my idol. In the early sixties there were but one or two women on the air at all the networks, and less than a handful behind the scenes in management or production. I was ambitious and smart and even though the brass at ABC liked me I was "kept in place." Today they call it the "glass ceiling." Then it was more like a maze with no exit. The only way a woman could crack the maze if she was very lucky was to become a researcher. I didn't have a degree at the time, so without brains on paper, or a father who was a Lord, I was out of the loop.

My boss, the Executive Producer was tough but fair and he went to bat for me to get Associate Producer credits on shows I worked tirelessly on. The big boys upstairs actually devoted brain cells to whether or not I could get a credit. "Patsy is terrific, she's an enormous asset, but we have to consider contracts and unions, blah, blah, blah." I finally got Assistant to the Producer. That pesky helper thing again.

I don't think the researcher thing was for me, anyway. The one gal I knew in that job was as weird as a three dollar bill. She was fixated on Mao and the Cultural Revolution and carried the Little Red Book around. Now and then we'd go to lunch and she'd spout all this Chinese jargon. I didn't know what in the hell she was talking about, so I guess on some level I was too normal.

Lady Rachel continued to breeze in and out in the high suede boots like Brenda Starr on a mission. My part in her network experience ended and off she went, back to England, the BBC, and daddy.

A few years before I met Rachel I spent some time in Europe, including Ireland. At the time I didn't make the connection but she was a Longford and they own a whole county in Ireland, swiped from the peasants in one of the many British land grabs.

Six or seven years later, home now with a baby, I'm reading the Sunday New York Times. Then I come across an article by Lady Rachel Longford. The little blurb says, "daughter of Lord Longford of County Longford, Ireland, sister of Antonia Frasier." Antonia Frasier, the well-known biographer of British Royalty is married to Harold Pinter, the eminent playwright. The article is a coming of age story of her experiences in New York, some of it at ABC News. As the dog pooped on the rug and the baby cried to be fed I was flushed with a resentment and anger at her ease of passage. The Lady Rachel I once knew seemed a discombobulated stranger in a strange land, but a well connected one, now in glossy glory in the NY Times. And me, well I never made it out of the maze. Oh, and no, she didn't mention my name.

# A 1950's Gal in the Newsroom

Into a useless space
they inserted her.
A filler,
for continuity's sake.
Idle eyes and ears
contemplate ingenuity –
hoping to rescue what's
left of her clan.

She borrows their
leftover time –
to assist them in a
reproduction. The
Scores of War
in two dimensions.

Gender duties and
grace; form a  minor
distraction –
and thins out the
competition –
Too bad,
in twenty years,
they'll know better.

An inaugural thought,
could jumpstart
a stagnant career,
but starting over is easier.

# *Teacher*

He said, "I talk –
you listen"

this old gray man, with a shaky voice,
pouring his wisdom in me.
pale, dried, folds of skin,
racing to meet each other.

He said, "I show –
you watch"

his freckled spots, no longer pink,
now, this dull beige on gray.
hair; silver white, greased up high,
climbing to touch its youth.

He said, "I give –
you take."

this bent over walk, stick like legs;
a voice, too weak to shout.
hands that shake, lips that curl,
thoughts that fly the wind.

He said, "I go –
you wait"

a slowed up heart, gasping for air
lungs, too weak to breathe.
a body laid out, quiet and calm
a soul, down in the ground.

I said, "You go –
I'll wait!"

# *Painted Ladies*

I watched in dismay as the paint flowed down each carpeted stair. Like a waterfall in slow motion, it crested at the edge of each step before cascading over to the next one. The silliest thought came to mind – *and the paint is blue like water.*

"Lyn," I screamed, "Look what I did!" "Oh, God, Rita, what happened?"

"I knocked the whole can of paint on the stairs. Nothing will take that out. It's ruined! Mr. C will fire us before we even start." In a panic I tried mopping up the globs of blue disaster. It was useless.

Whatever possessed me to enter this field of work at my age? To paint houses? I was 50 years old! Since I had my children and saw to it they were raised and praised and out on their own, I hadn't worked outside the home for years. Here I was at Lyn's friendly coercion, painting the whole inside of a seven room home!

Lynda Lewis was the exact opposite of me; a tall, pretty blonde with fair, Nordic features to my average height, and olive complexioned Italian looks. My neighbor before becoming my friend, Lyn was accustomed to manual labor. Long before she retired, she worked for a housing development company, where she learned plumbing, building handicap ramps, repairing walls and much, much more. It made sense for

189

her to think about a venture like this. I wasn't sure about my part in it, though.

"Come on, Rita," she cajoled, "You're good at painting, I'm good at striping. I'll teach you to stripe, you show me how to paint." Striping was another part of this new job offer- striping parking lots. "What do you say? We can do this, I know we can." But as I sat in the cozy safety of my cheerful blue and white kitchen, I was hesitant. I never would have dreamed of attempting such a feat. My resumé, if I had one, would have revealed a short stint as a telephone operator, a bank bookkeeper, a stay-at-home mom. But Lyn had me hooked... Two women venturing into this male dominated field. And we entered into it with a sense of fun.

We called ourselves The Painted Ladies.

* * *

We were on our first job in Clark, N. J. , and already a disaster had occurred. We cleaned up the mess as best we could, which only made it worse. I dreaded Mr. C's arrival. He was going to stop in after work. Meanwhile, Lyn and I spackled and sanded and painted another room. "Rita, I want this job, but don't worry about it; if he fires us, so be it." Lyn tried to calm me down, but I felt bad. She had three children, two still at home, and I knew that as a single mom she could use the money. Her ex was sporadic in his child support, and she was too proud to go after him for it. For awhile she hosted at the Lincroft Inn to supplement her meager income.

My worry was unfounded. I led Mr. C to the painted carpet and he merely laughed. "Rita, this rug is coming up-don't waste another thought on it." As he looked around at the newly coated room, he said, "I like your work so far, ladies. The persimmon color looks great in this room." Our first compliment!! He handed us two sleeping bags. "Since there is no furniture in the place, I took these from my boat. I figured they'd be more comfortable than the floor." Lyn and I had already decided to stay in the empty house, rather than travel back and forth from the shore. I eyed the bags with trepidation – this was another first.

We had electricity, heat, and running water, but there were no curtains on the windows. "Turn that lamp off, Lyn, you want to give the neighbors a show?" I was tired after a full day's work, and was even looking forward to the sleeping bags. Lyn, however was almost six foot tall, and didn't think she'd fit in one. We had to undress and dress in the dark, fumbling with our clothing and giggling at the absurdity of it. After the first day, or rather night, we knew our way around in the darkness. "Why the hell do people go camping?" I grumbled to Lyn. "These damn sleeping bags are so uncomfortable!"

Mr. C brought us a meal every other night. This was not in the job description, and we figured he could keep an eye on us by having an excuse to come by so often. He was a pleasant, nice-looking guy in his thirties, with a good sense of humor. He seemed amused, but pleased at our progress; so pleased that he gave us a new paint sprayer to make the job easier. Lyn and I took it outside to learn how to use it, and in doing so, got into a spray fight. Good thing it was latex paint that comes off with water!

In the evening, after showering and eating, we would order out, and picnic on the floor. Lyn brought along a deck of cards, and we played rummy to wind down before hitting the dreaded sleeping bags. Those bags weren't the best things for old bones; I awoke in the morning with more aches and pains than the job caused.

We were finished after five days, and looked forward to getting back to our families. Mr. C paid us handsomely, more than our original agreement. We were proud of what we'd done, and he appreciated it. With this first job under our belts, we were on our way!

Lyn's sister was a freelance artist in Manhattan, and sketched out a cute oversized business card for us. It featured two Victorian ladies in ballerina attire, splattering paint brushes in hand. People got a kick out of the cards, for they didn't pretend that we were young *or* sexy. They didn't have perfect figures- they were just like us! Our business signs were done in hot pink, and the pylons we 'borrowed' from some road construction were painted over in hot pink, also. Word of mouth spread; we were neat, and our prices were lowered for senior citizens and the handicapped, which was a great selling point.

I liked going home at night and pointing to my hair or clothing, showing my husband the colors we painted in a living room, bathroom, or bedroom. I wore my colors proudly!

\* \* \*

"That woman is a bitch!" Lyn was indignant. We were on a job in Rahway, staining and sealing an outside deck. She was angry for me; I had to go to the bathroom, but the woman wouldn't let me use her john; there was a gas station down the block and I should go there. I was embarrassed and angry, but since we were in the middle of the work, there was nothing to do but walk to the station. There were so many things we could have done to sabotage the work; not putting the seal down correctly, so water would seep in and ruin the wood, or not scrape the paint on the posts well and it would peel at the first sign of bad weather. But in spite of the lady of the house's behavior, Lyn and I did a good job and left, thankful to be gone from there.

One of the dirtiest jobs we ever did was in a so-called respectable neighborhood. We took the job gladly for the house outside was beautiful. "Holy cow" I whispered to Lyn. "Look at the floor!" The woman was putting out her cigarettes on the floor. In the corner of the kitchen was dog feces; not fresh, but dried and hard. We had to clean the mess before we could paint- it was disgusting! As we moved the furniture out of the way, there were more surprises; bits of food on the floor were attracting ants! As we painted, we were picking insects off the walls. When we were almost finished, (Thank goodness, we thought) Mrs. A asked us to paint the stairway to the cellar. There were shelves along the side walls, being used as a pantry. While Lyn and I were removing the canned goods, we looked at each other; the smell was unbearable. Some of the cans had been opened and put back- with food left in them. There was mold, and we found nails and screws mixed in the opened cans. "I can't wait to get home and scrub myself clean," Lyn whispered to me.

\* \* \*

On the bright side, one job was so pleasant we hated to see it end. Mrs. J would seat us in the Florida room, a cheery room with floor to ceiling windows, a glass-topped table and wrought-iron chairs. Though Lyn and I were clean, our clothes were paint spattered, and we didn't want to be in this pretty room. Mrs. J would serve us orange juice and coffee in the morning, and it was there we had our lunch, too. She made us eat our sandwiches on china plates and drink from crystal glasses. "There is no reason not to enjoy nice things, even when you're working," she would say. She was a lovely lady. So nice, in fact, that we bleached the mold from one side of the house, no charge. Mrs. J was so grateful that she added another task- to paint the garage floor! This was something we'd never done before, but Lyn and I decided we could do this. At the hardware store, we told Gary, the owner, what the job was, and asked his advice. He gave us what we needed, told us how to go about it, and we added another level to our profession. Mrs. J gave us a hundred dollar tip!

Lyn and I continued our endeavor for close to eight years, and though I was enjoying myself, I traded one job for another; taking care of my granddaughters so my daughter could go back to work. I went from painting to Pampers.

# One on One

He called me funny–
Ain't that a bitch!
as if, that's what I wanted to hear.
I poured out my soul and
showed him my drawers
and he says–
I made him laugh.

He's got that
funky laugh, too–
make you smell beans
whenever he breathes.
holds his stomach
and pats your back,
like your lives
ain't been intimate.

I didn't have the guts
to tell him the truth–
that my shit wasn't
meant to be funny.
I just lied
on my back
and took that crap
and told him–
I found it funny, too.

# A Bad Review

It didn't sound any better –
second time around.
Words don't age
like vintage grapes.

If I were able –
to simply walk away,
the point would be moot.

My fear, is that
there's no place –
No *better* place.
Which is quite sad, cause
this place sucks.

you should've seen his face.
it mirrored his mind.
he tried to wipe it off – that
winter's smile.

Then – there's an awkward silence,
the flashing kind.
yellow neon sign says,
*"approach with caution"*.

the skill –
is how to get away –
no break, no sound.
just a new thought.

and no new words,
cause that would be cheating.
besides, he knows
brilliance when he hears it.

# *The Stranger*

His constant stare pierced a hole in Celia Stewart's mind. She kept wondering where she'd seen him before. An alluring gaze that started the moment she arrived in the boarding area. He scanned her up and down, studied her face, her clothes and then her body. Celia kept moving looking for a seat to get away. She checked her buttons and her zipper. All were secure. She glanced at her reflection in the café's polished chrome. There were no hairs sticking wildly in the air. So, Celia Stewart calmly continued looking for a seat, having settled the question of her personal hygiene.

A woman removed her bag from the seat beside her. Celia accepted the invitation sitting behind the gate ramp and facing towards the stranger. His eyes still followed.

She considered returning a gentle smile, but she wasn't yet flattered. Though he was quite handsome, his look was far too cool and distant, as if it was she who had stared at him and he was merely returning the gaze. But every time she glanced up, his eyes were there – looking through her, suspending time for that brief moment.

Passengers bustled about temporarily blocking his view. He stepped back and peered over a man shorter than him. This time, Celia stared back. She stared hard assessing every corner of his perfect persona. He was casual and confident, as though the whole world knew him, but dared not approach.

He whispered something private to the gate agent. Her soft giggle and covered mouth told Celia he was a player. He had on a deep sage suit that went well with his black shirt and striped tie. His entire ensemble was a perfect blend of olive, sage, black and white. He was the cover of GQ.

Flight 477, Evansville to Pittsburgh was finally called for boarding. As the line moved, he let others pass in front of him, preoccupied by Celia's location. But she stayed back waiting for her boss who'd been traveling with her. She hesitated just long enough for others to fill the space between them. The stranger kept glancing behind himself over and over. His eyes followed Celia all the way to her seat. He even nodded as she passed.

Celia struggled harder for recollection. He acted as though they knew each other, but she couldn't figure out why. She was tired. Too tired to think. It had been a two week trip that left her exhausted and glad to head home. The elaborate dinner last night was long and boring. A five course meal with ten other researchers; none of whom shared a single common trait with Celia. They were white, men, 40's, with a passion for golf and skiing; two topics that consumed the entire evening's conversation. Celia's boss kept interjecting with stupid questions to which he already knew the answers. "Celia do you ski? Have you even been to Aspen? You play golf, right?" She wasn't sure if he was trying to isolate her or draw her in. "I'm going to have to get you out on the course with me sometime. I've seen her throw a softball," he told the others. "I bet this gal could swing a club." Their exhilaration filled the table. And as always, Celia smiled humbly, lowered her head and pretended to be grateful for the inclusion.

Suddenly, this clear memory of last night's dinner reminded Celia where she'd seen the stranger before. It was at the restaurant. He was sitting two tables over with three other men. They were laughing and animated, drawing on cocktail napkins. And they were all far too focused to remember their magnetic badges clipped to the outside pockets of their finely tailored Pierre Cardin suits. Celia's staring stranger was a fellow employee.

She wondered what he did and who he was. What job did he

have that allowed him to be so polished?  Her lab attire was always plain and subdued; flat shoes and long skirts accented by a blue un-tapered lab coat embossed with her name.  But everything about the stranger including the company he kept said he was "downtown;" sales, marketing or finance; the people who pushed her buttons.

Drinks and snacks had started coming through the aisle.  A young black woman filled a glass with too much ice and too little coke and then handed it to Celia's boss.  He was perturbed, as always; immediately ready to start his soliloquy on airline miserliness.  Rob Carlson could fill a two hour silence with his dissertation on beverages, peanuts and frequent flyer rules.  He took in a deep breath, but the woman interrupted, "would you like the whole can, sir?"

"Absolutely, thank you."

Celia and Rob nodded to each other a virtual toast.  He had won a small victory, either by his  word of mouth or his periodic written campaigns.  In either case, USAir was doling out entire cans of soda.

Celia was quickly ready with her order.   Her usual ginger ale – no ice and no-thank you to the peanuts.  But before she could speak, the young woman reached across and handed Celia a folded piece of paper.  "From the gentleman up front," she whispered.  "Would you like something to drink?"

Rob's eyes followed the flight attendant and studied Celia as she began unfolding.  A knot suddenly twisted in her stomach either from anticipation or humiliation.  She'd figure out which, a little later.  Her eyes stared at the words, but nothing registered.  She could only feel Rob's presence on her neck, peering over her shoulder trying to sneak his peek.  "Something to drink, Ma'am?"

"Huh?  Oh, yes please.  Uhm.  Uhm.  Ginger ale, please." She turned the paper face down, completely oblivious to the tons of ice being scooped into the cup.  The flight attendant handed her the cup, the can and two bags of peanuts.

"What was that?  You got a note from somebody?"

"Yea, ah, just a friend of mine up front."

"I didn't realize you knew anybody on this flight.  Who is it?" Rob had no qualms about prying.  He considered Celia his charge and protégé.  Whatever she was doing was completely his business.  "Where's he sitting?"

She watched Rob stretch his neck looking around, trying to identify a likely companion. She read the note:

Would you be interested in meeting for a drink? There's a pub just outside the concourse. Hope to see you there.                    Wade.

Rob's attention quickly turned back to Celia, still trying to read over her shoulder. "Is something wrong?"

"It's nothing. Nothing. My friend just needs a ride."

"Oh." Rob wasn't at all satisfied with the lack of intrigue. He knew there was more, but he couldn't figure out how to be bolder.

The ginger ale was cold and sent shivers through Celia's chest. She sipped some more and swirled it around. She hated peanuts and the smell of them around her. "I asked for no ice."

A different flight attendant came by to pick up empty cups and garbage. Celia handed her the half finished can of soda, the peanuts and the cup of ice. "Did you get your note?" she asked.

Celia nodded quickly trying to shoo her away. It seemed the entire crew knew about her note. Rob looked up from his newspaper but was unaware of the exchange.

The flight landed at 5:30; twenty minutes past it's schedule arrival. Rob told Celia he'd see her tomorrow, unaware the day was Friday. "Yea, see you tomorrow." She took her time departing the plane and headed straight for the bathroom. She knew Rob would wait and watch, but with a good 10 minutes in the ladies room, he'd wisely head home.

The pub was down a small rotunda at the end of the concourse. Wade stood at the bar, drink already in hand. Celia paused a moment to wonder why she was there.

"Hello, I don't think we've met. I'm Celia Wilson. Do you work at Reynolds Steel?"

"Actually, we have met and yes I do work at Reynolds Steel." He shook Celia's hand fast and firmly.

"I'm sorry, I don't remember."

"At the Reynolds Black Caucus Dinner about two months ago. You were sitting with Karen Johnson, or Karen Ramsey as she's now known. She introduced us, but I guess you don't remember. I've never made such a dull impression on a woman before. I'll have to polish up my act."

"Too much wine, I suppose. I'm sorry I wasn't more alert. Anyway, it's nice to meet you. Again."

"Would you like a drink?"

"Ginger ale will be good. Maybe I'll remember you, this time." Celia felt sure they hadn't met, but she was indeed sitting with Karen that night.

Wade Armstrong was a Finance Director with an office downtown. He had gone to school at Penn State but swore he'd never settle down in Pennsylvania. He was a California boy and Pennsylvania was much too slow. But since stable jobs were hard to find, Pittsburgh became his home.

He'd been at Reynolds Steel two years longer than Celia and seemed to know everyone she knew. He was the chairman of the Black Caucus and tried to make it a point to meet everyone. But Celia knew this was not his normal meeting style.

The knot in her stomach turned tighter, as he directed her to a small table. He sat across from her staring once again. His eyes, a light pearl brown, did not seem to go with his dark skin. And he held them on Celia seemingly for minutes without turning away. Celia on the other hand, could not hold the eye contact. She lowered her head, stared at her drink or anything else that would untwist her knot. She asked him questions, he gave her answers; each time burying his motives beneath the response.

An hour had passed before Celia remembered her large suitcase with two weeks of laundry. Though her knot had never untwisted, the flattery had stimulated so many other parts of her body, she no longer cared about the pain in her gut. She rushed away to baggage claim after scribbling her number on a napkin. Whether or not he ever called, the stimulation had been worth the time.

Monday morning came all too quickly. Two cups of tea had

not opened Celia's eyes or her mind. Despite two days off and a sweet October weekend, Celia still felt that traveler's drag.

Her lab was white and steel, sterile and dull. But today it was adorned by a single red rose – delivered to her desk at 9:00 am. The fragrance followed her through the room. It reminded her of his eyes. And all the empty spaces left her mind; the ones she used to use for experiments and equations, were now filled with thoughts of him. Work moved slowly.

When her phone rang and it was him, she remembered being fifteen.

The anticipation of dinner used up the rest of her day. It was her first taste of Jazz that was not Miles Davis. It was a small club in Shadyside right on Walnut Street. A hip place to be. She met his friends and even the band leader. Tasted her first martini.

On Tuesday, Karen Ramsey invited her to lunch. She was meeting her old friend Robin who had just landed a job as executive assistant to Tom Harvey, President of Research. Karen insisted they pick up Robin at her desk. She couldn't wait for the chance to see inside the president's office.

Robin sat at her desk smiling from ear to ear. Celia and Karen were completely in awe. The wood paneling and hand carvings were truly impressive. Robin's desk was huge and sat right in the middle of the room. A large door behind her was open, allowing bright streams of light to burst through. Celia peeked in, gawking at the mahogany desk and the leather couch. She sat in Robin's chair waiting for Karen to complete her tour.

Robin's desk was meticulous. Pads and pens in perfect position. No stray papers or clips. Photos aligned in a row. Gorgeous photos, like the ones you take in glamour shops. Family photos like the ones you take at Christmas time. Wade Armstrong's photo – like the one he took on their wedding day.

# A Career Change

all I want is my freedom back –
some time on my hands.
rustle it through my fingertips,
let some drip down my arms.
maybe even thicken it up,
make a pomade to
straighten out my curls.

I want to get rid of that crinkle
in my forehead.
doubt is folded up
in there and now I've got this permanent scar.
– guess if I tan a little, they won't see it.

I want to get my feet fixed too – years
of running, chasing and kicking
bent up my toes – I'm starting to
walk bent over –  which was OK
for back then, but
now, I want to look tall.

spend some time being artistic –
maybe even bleed a little.
add a splash of pigment,
to an ancient genre –
like the sway of Togo dancers
at a Carolina cotillion.

and of course, I've got to travel.
press my nose against the window –
watch the suns off two
horizons – then tan deep and dark.
maybe visit the Holy
Land or hike in West Virginia.
I'll stay away from water sports, though –
they tend to put the curl
back in my hair.

### ❦

# *The Lab*

She was not a pleasant woman to be around. Dorothy Mason was only happy when she was insulting or embarrassing her co-workers, and unassuming Alex was usually her scapegoat. He was the most serious, hardworking guy in the laboratory. He loved his job, though the others thought it monotonous, putting samples of various particles under a microscope to see how they reacted to certain variables.

Ms. Mason always belittled Alex's size. He was a short man, bespectacled, with nothing remarkable about him. His 5' 4" frame was topped by a homely face and thus became the butt of the woman's jokes. Yet Dorothy seemed unaware of her own flaws. She was obese, her walk a waddle. Her peroxide blonde hair was thinning due to the many bleachings it had withstood. Dorothy thought herself fashionable, and wore the latest styles, all of which looked ridiculous on her. The short skirts showed her dimpled cellulite; not a pretty picture. And the tank tops she dared wear showed her middle bulge to the world.

"Hey, Shorty, stop staring at my knees. Oh, you're not, that's how tall you are." And she giggled at her weak joke. Alex tried to ignore her, but it was difficult. The cutting jibes, "hey, does your ass hit the curb when you step down?" were taking their toll.

One late afternoon prior to closing the lab, Dorothy noticed that Alex looked furtively around and put something in his private safe. Her curiosity piqued, she waddled over to his counter singing "Short people got no body. Watcha trying to hide there, short stuff?"

Alex flushed and replied primly, "nothing, I'm merely putting today's work away." His hand shook though, as he locked the safe. The lights in the sterile white room were systematically being turned off, throwing the room into shadowy shades of gray. The heavy woman lingered until everyone had gone. She didn't believe for one minute that the little man wasn't hiding something. Dorothy approached his safe and bent to open it. She knew the combinations to all the staff's safes; by watching carefully she had memorized them all.

As she studied the papers she thought, "looks like Tattoo's working on something of his own." The plan seemed to be a latex based formula. "Have to keep an eye on this. I wonder what he has in mind?"

As weeks passed Alex was more and more excited about something, but he was still very secretive. Ms. Mason saw him stretch a substance which looked like a taffy pull. That night, after everyone had gone home, she opened the safe again and found what seemed like a piece of rubber, soft and pink and so pliable, the woman sighed at the feel of it. It felt warm and almost alive in her chubby little hands. An idea came to her. This stuff would make a wonderful girdle, soft and giving yet strong enough to hold a stomach in comfortably.

She stayed late into the night working the material into a round, barrel-like circle. Dorothy had no qualms about stealing Alex's formula. As she pressed the strange substance into shape, the seams disappeared; it became one smooth piece. It was wonderful! In great anticipation the greedy woman shed her clothes and wriggled into the rubberized thing. It held her bulging stomach in perfectly. Dorothy paraded around the lab preening at the slim shape the girdle gave her. In just minutes she felt constricted; at first uncomfortable, then painful. The stuff was shrinking on her body! Panicked, she tried to peel it off, but it was like a second skin, suffocating her, taking her breath away.

Dorothy didn't see Alex peeking around a corner, smirking at her death throes as she screamed, " My girdle is killing me!!"

# Demons

## *Just Breathe*

She left the restaurant on a hot summer night, chilled to the bone, walking alone along the dark streets of Asbury Park. The anger, fear, and hurt that fueled her steps were ignited by the ice blue rage in her daughter's eyes. Patsy passed the chicken take out joints, the dollar stores, the Salvation Army, the dingy bars, her feet slipping in her little black sandals. She left her family there just as coffee was being served. She left her family there at her husband's birthday dinner, too broken to smile and laugh it off, too exhausted by her daughter's emotional roller coaster to pacify, to back off, to take the slap.

They were an animated group, laughing and conversing freely, a good family, a family once beset by the tragic toll of alcoholism many years before. That pain seemed a distant echo, distant yet still reverberating like some inner tuning fork in the lives of their children, now adults in their thirties. But here they were here bantering with a quick wit, sharing a laugh, catching up with the news. When the subject turned to the war in Iraq, Lisa offered a pithy comment, "My shrink says that Bush is on a dry drunk." Patsy, with a quick retort, said, "Oh, is that the same shrink who blames your mother for everything?" A second of silence froze the air just as the world tilted with Lisa's fury. "I've had enough. I won't let you get away with that. You are to blame!!!"

Stunned, silenced, Patsy shuddered, her hands shaking, her face flushed. She walked outside for some air, then just kept walking. When she finally found a cab to take her home she retreated to the back yard, lights off, hiding alone in the dark. When Tom found her she said, "I don't want to see her, to talk to her. Just take her to the next train to New York." Her son came back to say, "We're leaving." His wife was the only soft one, hugging her gently before they left, "It'll be all right, Patsy."

Patsy usually trod gently with Lisa, backing off from her quick retorts, avoiding confrontation, yet always available for her emotional meltdowns, fewer since she was married, but he wasn't there tonight. She was a fury with beauty and brains, a formidable talent whose artistic visions in a cutthroat world created chaos as she trolled through the mean streets of the city and the day glow light of LA. Patsy was her buffer, her lady knight of rescue.

*"I don't deserve this. I've always been there for her, always. I can't win. I never can win with her. She was just waiting, waiting to vent and one wise remark was all it took. I can't do this anymore. It's over. It's just over. Let her go. Let her go home to Kevin. Oh, he'll hear it all. He'll be okay with me, I think. I hope so. I love him. She's a lucky woman. I can't even talk about this. When Tom gets back he'll let me be. He knows. It hurts him when I'm hurt, but he knows. He's seen it before. Maybe I'll just sit out here all night. I don't care anymore, I can't do this anymore."*

But her heart was broken for she knew the truth; the cold reality of those terrible years when her scotch fueled brain and breath terrified her daughter. *"I've been sober for fifteen years. I made amends. We've talked and talked. Will it never end?"*

The next day, then another, and another passed. Patsy was immobilized, deeply wounded and frightened that the rift had widened like a canyon from their emotional earthquake. Their conversation when it came blew like hot ashes across the wires, singeing as her throat dried, too choked to argue any more. Lisa let her know, let her know how deeply those years scrambled her. Lisa let her know how hard she had worked on herself to leave the trauma of alcoholic parents in the dust. Still, Patsy stuttered, "I love you, I've done everything I could for you." Lisa said, "I love you too, Mom. It actually hurts me that I have a life of an artist, a life you never had." For Lisa knew all too well of the deep chasm of grief and emptiness that nearly drowned her mother in alcohol.

But like victims of a raging fire, now quieted for so many years, the soft pink scars would always be branded in her heart.

Then, breathing in and breathing out was all they agreed to do for Patsy wasn't ready, wasn't ready to dig into the deep black coal pit of pain when she saw herself like a shadow figure, a doppelganger of destruction. And yet she knew the umbilical cord of life, so strong and yet so fragile needed the juice of forgiveness between mother and daughter. Then, she used the small gift of her pen to open the space, the breathing space so choked by the fumes of the past. When Lisa received her letter she called and said, "Thank you, Mom."

This morning they are cuddled on a bed, Lisa's head in her mother's lap, her face warm, Patsy's hands gently passing over her child's brow, smoothing her soft silky hair. It is a quiet moment, an intimate moment, then Lisa just says, "Mommy."

# *Shadows of Fear*

As she ducked into the little shop, anyone would have thought it was merely to get out of the rain that decorated the streets with pock marks of baby splashes. Dee was damp all right, but it was more of a cold sweat. Inside her jacket, damp patches were already staining her underarms, and she felt the trickle of perspiration working its way down her back and between her breasts. The feeling had come over her again; someone was following her. She felt something nudge against her.

"Oops. Sorry! Oh, hi Dee, I didn't see you. Daydreaming, I guess."

Dee, heart pounding, looked around to see Jimmy, her sister's friend. "Oh, it's you. I didn't see you, either."

"Nasty weather, huh? How have you been? Haven't seen you in awhile."

"Well, between work and stuff, I don't have much of a social life," Dee replied. She wasn't about to tell him about her sad love life, etc.

"Must get moving, see you around." And the young man walked out.

Dolores Woods, better known affectionately as Dee, a 27 year old computer service assistant, was a young woman who enjoyed her job, friends, and family. She was a pretty girl who didn't know she was pretty. She was just coming down from a broken relationship, and was wary of starting another, so her job and pets took up her time. Dee shook out her shoulder length auburn hair, throwing out little droplets of rain. Her hazel eyes were clouded with worry; what was going on here? Why this dreadful feeling of danger and being followed?

She thought about seeing Jimmy. He was a policeman now, but Dee remembered him from school. He seemed nice enough. They bumped into one another every so often. The times seemed few and far between. She thought of a time, long ago, when Jimmy asked her out. Dee smiled to herself. She had let him down easy. He was more her sister's type.

The smell of cleaning fluid brought her back to the present, and looking around her, Dee realized it was a cleaners' she had hurried into. Since she had no clothes to leave, she felt foolish standing there. Sheepishly, she looked at the oriental woman behind the counter, who was looking at her expectantly.

"Sorry," she explained, "I thought this was the pet shop." Slowly she backed out of the store. *Have I gotten paranoid? Could I be imagining things?* These questions ran through Dee's mind and she tried to believe that the answer was yes, until she remembered the train of events that brought her to the conclusion that she was being stalked. The hang-ups when she answered the phone, things in her apartment that were moved or missing. She still couldn't find her favorite crystal heart-shaped paperweight. At first she thought she was mistaken, then forgetful. But then the feeling, irrational or not, said 'something's very wrong here.' Dee relied on her intuition, and it was screaming danger. When she told family and friends of her suspicions, they laughed at her good-naturedly, saying, "Dee, you have no enemies, everyone likes you; it's all in your mind." But the sensation of being watched was too strong to ignore.

The sky had finally stopped weeping, though the clouds were still angry. Dee decided to walk home in lieu of a taxi. On the way home, she stopped at Pet-Smart. She purchased dog biscuits for Georgie, her terrier, and liver treats for Puss. She loved her pets, and since there was no lover in her life at present, they were her close confidantes and she lavished them with love. The apartment was quiet as she entered the room. "Hey, guys, Mommy's home. Come say hello." Here came Puss, but where was Georgie, who barked at everything?

Suddenly her heart grew cold, as if ice water ran through her veins. *NO,* Dee thought, *nononono.* A feeling of dread flowed over her. As she walked into the kitchen, the smell of burnt fur assailed Dee. There was her little Georgie lying near the stove, dead. Her mind told her, *this was no coincidence. This was cruelty. Someone got in here- how? Who? If I call the police, they won't believe me. I have no proof.*

Dee remembered then that Jimmy was on the force. He might help her, especially since they had just met again this afternoon. She got through to him and he rushed right over. As he entered the apartment, he exclaimed," Are you all right? What's that smell?" Dee explained the situation; he believed her! *Thank God,* Dee thought. *Someone who doesn't think I'm crazy.* The young, good-looking policeman listened to Dee's tale and calmed her down. He helped her wrap Georgie in a sheet and promised to bury the poor burnt pup. Jimmy suggested that she leave town for awhile, for this last act of cruelty made her stalker dangerous. He also suggested that she not tell anyone where she was going. He would investigate anyone and everyone she knew, and give her the okay to come home when it was safe. Dee agreed and they worked out a plan as to where she should go. She told her family she was taking some of her vacation time and going away to rest. Her mom took Puss, after she explained to her that Georgie was staying at her friend Betty's; she couldn't bear to talk about him to anyone. Now Dee was free to go.

She had a fake I.D. from college days, so Dee used it and bought a ticket to a far destination. She was now Rachel Williams. She chose California, a world away from her home town. She looked forward to the salty air, salt water taffy, sand in her shoes. When she checked into her beach front apartment, she paid a month in advance. *How long must I be incognito?* She wondered. *For as long as it takes,* her mind echoed back.

Dee sat at the ocean's edge, watching the waves come in and slide back out, dragging bits of shells and flotsam in its wake. Her two piece bathing suit was a modest cut, a sea green color, complimenting her hazel eyes. She felt at peace this past week, thousands of miles separating her from her problem at home. Relaxed and already tanned, in the serenity of this peaceful setting Dee wondered at times if she had been dreaming the whole stalking affair. She loved it here at the shore. Seeing the morning sun reflect on the water, which mirrored its golden orb, started her day. At the end of the day, she would watch the sun set lower and lower until it kissed the ocean goodnight before disappearing into its depths.

There were people all around her on the beach. Dee was among a multitude of strangers. Jimmy had advised this, saying there would always be witnesses nearby, and a stalker would be hard-pressed to do her any harm. If once in awhile she had that old feeling of being watched, well, she probably was with so many people around.

Eyes closed, face tilted up to welcome the sun, Dee relaxed and let the warmth envelope her. When a hand touched her shoulder, she swallowed a scream. Panicked, she looked at the owner of the hand.

"Excuse me, miss, your flip-flops are floating away."

She took a deep breath, let it out, and tried a shaky smile at the young man in front of her

"Thank you so much; I was zoned out, I guess." And she reached down, plucking her flip-flops from the water. After he nodded to her, and walked away, Dee had second thoughts. *Was that really a good Samaritan? Were my flip-flops really in the water, or did he put them there while I daydreamed? Is he the stalker?* After a moment of fear, she shook her head. No, she was being foolish. This was nothing to worry about. So she relaxed and breathed easy once more.

Dee was a good swimmer, and one morning she swam out past the boundary ropes. It was a lovely solitary feeling being out there and she floated, eyes closed, enjoying her aloneness. Suddenly something grabbed her from beneath the water, dragging her down and under. She panicked, spluttered, but fought with all her might, kicking and swinging her arms at whatever held her. Just when she thought her burning lungs would burst, Dee kicked out and landed a hard blow to her assailant. She was free! Upon reaching the shore she fell feebly on the sand, retching. *What was that? What's happening to me? <u>Why</u> is it happening to me? Call Jimmy, call Jimmy.* So a very frightened Dee called Jimmy. He said, "Hang on kid, I'll be there tomorrow. Try not to panic."

He arrived on Friday, and Dee looked at him, her savior. "Jim, I can't take much more of this!" she cried, wringing her hands. "I don't understand why this person is stalking me, and now he's trying to hurt me!" They were sitting in the dark on the beach that evening, hearing

218

but not seeing the ocean's waves; their rolling in and slipping out in the natural rhythm of thousands of years.

"You won't have to, Dee," Jimmy answered. His tone of voice sounded strange. A chill ran down her spine. "You got away from me yesterday with that lucky kick. I didn't think you had it in you." He reached for her and before she could scream his hands were around her throat, choking the life out of her. Jimmy knew Dee's face was turning purple, her eyes pleading, questioning; WHY? He was happy to comply.

"I've watched you for years, Miss High and Mighty. Do you forget when I asked you years ago for a date and you blew me off, laughing? Well, I never forgot. You became an obsession. I couldn't stand to see you with anyone else, it ate me up inside. I couldn't stand to see you happy when I was so miserable. Nobody can have you now. And nobody knows where you are, or that I know where you are." He chuckled eerily.

Dee stopped breathing, and in the darkness of the night Jim swam out with her body and let the undertow carry her to wherever its destination lay. Now he could leave for home, at peace with himself at last. He fondled the little crystal paperweight in his pocket, as he walked off the beach whistling.

# *A Different World*

At 5:10 a.m. the sun had not yet risen. The secret hum of morning kept the birds silent and the crickets still. I moved cautiously through the old stone terminal. The only people there were those of us who had just arrived from New York City. The empty counters and dark cafés scared me. If a stranger made contact, there were no shops or stands to loiter near; no official uniforms to direct you to the exits. At five a.m., New York's Port Authority is already bustling with travelers. But I had never traveled alone in that terminal either.

I struggled to move from the gate to the exit. My shoulder bag and duffel bag hanging off the same shoulder. One hand gripped on my suitcase and the other on the old typewriter. The bus driver offered to carry the suitcase and duffel bag to the cab stand, but money was too tight to tip him. Knowing it wasn't an offer of kindness, I graciously said no thank you.

It only took 15 minutes to get to campus though I wanted it to take longer. It was too early to register. No one was around. No offices open. The few students that had already arrived slept quietly in their dorms awaiting the start of Summer Program. Most would arrive that day. They would pour in from vans and trailers packed to the brim. Mothers, fathers and siblings would unfold, primp and puff the precious belongings of their loved ones. Tears and last minute instructions would flow; pocket money checked, coins for laundry and calling home verified. And I would wonder, if they pitied me; un-puffed and un-primped, no parents or siblings to verify funds.

Though being alone and away from home is what I'd always dreamed of, I had no idea what to do. The improbability of this moment made planning seem ridiculous. But there I was, free to make the wrong decision, needing to do this right. Going back home was not an option.

A sign for program attendees pointed to a twelve story brick building, just off the main road. It's U-shape forced the rising sun to cast a cozy shadow onto the expansive courtyard. The pansies and lilies were bloomed, and the four o'clocks were still open, free from the morning heat. I sat close to the door, waiting for the admissions office to open.

The woman who finally came just before eight was young and bubbly. She greeted me warmly and helped bring my bags inside. It was my first experience with process. She told me which building was the Registrar, where to go for housing and how to pick a meal plan. Forms and papers, pink and blue, in triplicate copy cluttered my hands and mind. I needed a hand to hold, someone to watch me cross the street, those distant instructions; *close your legs when you sit, don't look strangers in the eye, keep your voice down in public.* How would I know what was right or wrong, given I'd never been led by my own thoughts.

The bubbly lady let me leave my bags behind her counter. A campus map with color coding guided my way. I found the gym and the dining hall. There was a small café called Skibo; a fast food alternative that accepted your dining points. The engineering and science buildings were parallel to each other with a long flowing lawn between them. I would later learn they called it the Cut. Soon, when fall session was in full swing, students would scatter the Cut; studying, bathing, reading, loving.

The Registrar's Office was near empty when I arrived. Short stout women stood at two counter windows each offering to help me. I chose the dark haired one with the softer voice. She called me Miss. The welcome pack was thick. A Rules and University policy document that had to be read and signed by each student. A list of instructor and counselor names. Supplies. Course descriptions and another map. Orientation would start at 1:00 p.m.

Things got easier once I found my dorm room, met my roommate and got my first campus meal. I was lucky to have the program scholarship with room and board. I had fifty five dollars and it would have to last for a while.

By noon, the dorm was crowded with other students and families. Their bounty astounded me; radios, record players, beautiful comforter sets, hangers and hangers of clothes. And the pity I predicted was my own. My tattered belongings were shameful and disheartening. I unpacked slowly so others couldn't study my wares. I waited for my roommates' family to leave before I made up my bed; adorned with hospital sheets and a moving blanket for warmth. I turned the Nassau County Medical emblem to the inside and tucked away the frayed edges of the blanket. Mommy's boyfriend, Henry had given us the blankets when he moved in with his mother's old furniture. I thought it odd that furniture needed a blanket, but it was the warmest one I'd ever had.

My Ohio roommate was named Shelia. We giggled for a while about Celia and Sheila. She was young like me; a high school junior singled out because she was good in math and science. But like the others, she was from a well-to-do family and a well-to-do town. Her high school had a swimming pool and tennis courts, small class sizes and teachers from ivy league schools. My town was small and poor. We had split school sessions because of overcrowding. Our brilliant students had all left for the specialized high schools, studying pre-medicine and pre-law. My mother's cynicism left me behind; longing for my peers, my brain starving for a challenge. I was petrified the moment Sheila unpacked her high school books. Calculus. Physics. Advanced chemistry. I didn't know what year she learned those things, I was just sure I'd never been taught them.

I told Sheila my master plan; to actually stay and become a freshman. She thought I was crazy. "Why would you want to stay," she asked. "Aren't you looking forward to your senior year; the parties, the prom, saying goodbye to all your friends, touring different universities?" She was right, why wouldn't someone want all those things? Surely I would, if they were ever possible.

I giggled long and slow, stalling to think of an answer. And I started to wonder whether this new world of people needed to know my shame. The had never heard my mother's discourse on the inevitable promiscuity of every young girl. They had never seen our family fights, my fathers belongings spread across the front yard, my mother's drunken stupor. They didn't know the shameful rumor of my birth or about the mystical mark beneath my eye. I realized if I hid my life carefully, I could appear to be just like them.

"Of course I'd miss my senior year," I told her. "But I came from a really small school. The prom isn't much to speak of. My father wants me to consider engineering and he really likes this school. He was all excited when we got here."

"Oh, wow. Where are your parents? Did they leave already? You guys must've gotten here real early."

"Yea, they headed back."

My four year series of lies and omissions had just begun. I would soon become the daughter of two loving parents, well educated siblings and a family history that dated back to Nigerian immigrants arriving at the Port of Baltimore. A splendid mix of fact and fiction that would send me to sleep each night almost believing I was cared for. Reality would only peek through when letters from home arrived or when the girls down the hall yelled out, "Celia, you have a phone call." It was always my mother, calling to tell me the latest Stewart family woes. *She threw Raymond out of the house again and caught Andrew smoking marijuana. She told Kevin she didn't want to see his newborn daughter. "That bastard child and her no-good mother aren't welcomed in my home!"*

There was no escaping who I was or from where I'd come. And there and then, I'd be required to pick a side. From four hundred miles away, it would once again be time to choose. Time to pick one distant kinship over another. *Raymond and Kevin were wrong, weren't they? Andrew was playing with fire, wasn't he?* And if I paused or hesitated, because my mind was consumed with calculus or physics, I too would be cursed and abandoned.

But in between those calls and letters, my illusions thrived. I told people my parents were still together, fighting over whose footsteps I would follow. Would I be an engineer like him, or a teacher like her? My brother Raymond was in graduate school but Hartford became Harvard. Pride in Vincent's Vietnam service only started when that rich girl from D.C. tried to out talk me in American History. Life had opened up, even if it was unreal.

I lived cautiously the first week. The world seemed even larger than I'd ever imagined and everyone else seemed to belong, but me. They were all so confident. Some were so brilliant, they couldn't speak or wouldn't speak; as if they had taken a vow of silence to avoid the unintelligent. The others had some secret, one I could never seem to share.

We took a test the second day. Everyone in a big concert-hall looking room. The brilliant well-to-do ones sped through it, page after page, looking as though they were insulted by the meager challenge. I crawled through each question, scratch papers everywhere, pulling from every childhood lesson.

On day three, we were assigned sections; Pre-Calc or Calculus 1, Physics or Advanced Mechanics, Introduction to Chemistry or Chem 1. A teaching assistant handed me a schedule: 9 a.m. Calc 1, followed by Advanced Mechanics, Creative Writing, lunch, South American History, Chemistry 1, plus a lab. I double checked to make sure she gave me the right schedule.

By week two, I had a little more pride in my tiny town. I realized I'd been taught well by some under-paid teachers and devoted counselors. The ones who met us at the community center when the union held a strike, but they couldn't bear to see us fall behind. The ones who used their own money for the Museum of Natural History trip when the board cut it out of the school budget. I was keeping up. I was more than keeping up. By week three, Dr. Oliver called me to his office and said they were offering me a scholarship to start as a freshman in September.

I had to keep it a secret until week four because I'd been asked outside of the normal process. I told no one, except my mother. She called again and I had to pick a side.

# No Donor Card

There are parts of you I miss.
I wish I could separate them out,
like a liver, or lung, or a kidney –
my friend needed one of those.
But you come in wholes.

Today,
a dozen violets – sweet,
wrapped in cellophane
and tied with a twist.

Today, a dozen violets;
but tomorrow, a fifth –

Funny how you damaged
the very parts I miss.

Tender harmonies from coral lips.
Lips now moistened moldy
by the brew.
They curse me now;

As do
the dark clouds your heart expelled –
a choking love; already dead.

Today,
a dozen violets;
but tomorrow, a fifth –

They tell me to savor what was sweet.
Dried violet petals, now
a powdery dust.
but with one good puff –

Your parts;
unusable now.
Too bad, too –
my friend needed some of those.
I miss him
in wholes.

# *Ritual Murder*

The double thick slick green plastic of the Hefty garbage bags stuck together as she rolled them out of the box. She tore the first one off, a silent zip in the night and though her hands were trembling her intent was clear. The kitchen counters were untidy. Stuck on spaghetti sauce, crust filled toaster, coffee grinds in the carafe, glasses in the sink ringed with soda, or milk, or wine. The quick franks and beans supper splattered brown freckles of goo in the microwave. It was time to clean.

She unplugged the toaster, opened a bag and dumped it. She did the same with Mr. Coffee. The mixer was next followed by the dirty dishes, glasses and cups. "Not enough," she thought, "not nearly enough." On the kitchen divider she eliminated the canisters and the first bag was filled.

The microwave was a large model and though she was able to move it to the edge of the counter, she could not manage to lift it to its demise. Frustrated, she left it cockeyed on the counter. She opened the utensil draw, a jumble of knives, forks, spoons, spatulas, a corkscrew, a turkey baster, nutcracker, birthday candles, and junk. Then she went to work on the cookbooks, cookie tins, pots and pans, followed by mixing bowls and the spice rack. It all went into bag number two. The garbage can that was beginning to smell filled bag number three.

Satisfied, she surveyed her handiwork. She had checked to insure that all the bedroom doors were closed. Then she opened the windows, turned on the gas and put her head in the oven.

If they heard her they didn't stir in the deep REM of three a.m.

# Sobering thoughts

Maybe just another drink
    will soft-pedal this thought
    pushing forward in my head
    of sinking lower than I ought.

I gave myself so freely
    to he who merely took
    me as lover, laundress
    mother, doctor, cook.

A drink or two will equal
    numbness, as it's done before
    to keep me slightly foggy
    and feeling neither-nor.

No, I will just stay sober
    to see life as it is
    and make a bid for freedom
    by letting him have his.

# *Who's There?*

      I look at the bed I didn't make today, the library books I didn't return, the bicycle I didn't ride, the phone calls I didn't make…Hello, hello, is anyone there? I know you are. Know it. Oh, yeah, you're just waiting as usual, playing tag with my head, lurking in the dark recesses of the jungle in my brain, holding tight for that bolt of lighting to force you open. Waiting, always waiting and I think, "Don't be mad at yourself, easy, easy, sit in the last rays of the fall, breathe, just breathe, try to be, try to be who you are." You're the only one watching. I see you beckoning, big and black and glistening, dripping my crystal tears on inlaid prisms of colored glass. I hear you, moaning softly, "Come to me, drown in me, love me."

      I know your tricks, you bastard. You like me vulnerable. You like me confused. You like me best of all when I'm hurt or sad or when I can't find my way. And when I'm tired or lonely you feed like a piranha stabbing me with self-doubt and hopelessness. You sick fuck.

      Patterns of the past do not erase easily. Their residue clings like the stink from the cigarettes I still smoke. Their memory substitutes coffee for scotch but not the fear, or the panic that still grabs at me, tingling my fingertips, staggering my footsteps as the spirals in my head claim me for an hour or a day. You paralyze me. You make me cry. You are harsh and cling like the slime that you are as I swat your rotting flies away day after day after day after day.

     The days are now years of footsteps each one leaving you further behind but never gone. I step out in the sun today to walk in the red and gold to the brilliant blue sea, choppy with fall's frosty caps of white. I embrace the beauty grateful for the gifts that keep you hidden in the subterranean depths of my core, the hot kernel of pain always waiting. You are me and I am you. Another day I say, "My name is Patsy, and I'm an alcoholic," and just for today you can knock, but you can't come in.

# *Sass*

# The Coupon Caper

I hate coupons. I hate the unending inundation of mail announcing special offers, weekly sales, one day only sales, midnight madness, early bird bonanzas. I hate the guilt that follows if I don't spend part of my morning sorting through these unsolicited intrusions of paper and catalogs that spawn like tadpoles, their glossy colored invitations slithering out of newspapers and envelopes. Why, I wonder do coupons still exist? Every time I use my bankcard my preference for Skippy or Hellmann's is surely recorded by a microchip, as is my taste in literature, music or fashion. If I can click three times and make a hotel reservation in Paris, why can't I just get the discount without the coupon? Sure I understand that the marketing and advertising gurus need to justify their existence to the "Where's the beef?" commercial God, and wonder if the market would crash if all the brain trusts, copywriters, graphic designers, printers and paper suppliers were suddenly out of a job.

To add to this huge annoyance to my sanity are those who catalogue these coupons alphabetically in a three by five index file and brag about their prowess of never missing a bargain. Now, I can't say that I don't try to get in the groove, I do, but I am just not up to the challenge. I stuff coupons in my purse, throw them on the front seat of my car, pack them in my pockets or squash them in the glove compartment waiting for the moment I can grab one of those little buggers at the right time and place. All to no avail. Prepping myself mentally and emotionally for the task at hand I arrive at the mega store to consumer consumption and begin to disassemble as I attempt to match the coupon to the product. I'm at the roller derby of shopping carts, bumping and getting bumped, but I have to slow down to read the small print.

> Save 50 cents on two packages. Void if altered, copied, sold, purchased, transferred exchanged or where prohibited or restricted by law. One coupon per purchase of specified products. Good only in USA. APO's & PPO's. No other coupon may be used with this coupon. Consumer pays any sales tax.

Then in really small print. Expires 12/3/06.

And so it goes, terminal tedium. Unmitigated disaster.

I began to shy away from the Coupon Queens, dreading the small talk that led to revelations of their monumental savings and indomitable quests. "I had a dollar coupon for Skippy's Peanut Butter, but they were all out, so they gave me a rain check, and I'll be back. Oh, yes, I'll be back. I just don't know why stores put things on sale and blah, blah, blah, blah, blah."

What was I to do? I had to fight back, get some respect, save money, be proud of my weekly grocery bill. And so I devised a system. I carefully chose certain items that were small but pricey. I then placed them in my shopping cart, but casually covered them with a scarf, a glove or my purse. These small but pricey items somehow swept out of the store with me, undetected by the cash registers electronic eye. This is a very good method for we all at one time or another have forgotten something in our shopping cart, and an innocent, "Oh, my gosh," could cover my scam. Come on now, fess up. A friend of mine innocently left with ten pounds of dog food in the bottom rack. My system was superb. I could save as much as $10 a heist. Just picture a bottle of Advil. Look at the price. Look at its size.

Oh, what bliss. I could now compete with the best of them. I, too, had saved $10 without even breaking a sweat, or pouring over the deritrous of all those poor dead trees. But, alas, my glory wasn't to last. Like so many felons who trip themselves up I began to share my secrets. This resulted in either looks of horror or shrieks of laughter, depending on the anal retentive degree of the listener as I recounted my exploits with Advil, cat food, batteries, mascara, a lipstick or two, paperbacks, toilet bowl cleaner and an occasional can of tuna.

Bravely I ventured on, though now a touch of paranoia was affecting my technique. Then, one day several policemen set upon a man who had just exited the supermarket. They handcuffed him and took him away. I carefully placed my purloined items in the basket. My caper was over.

# The Three Witches

Maddie, the Earth Mother, had fattened up in recent years. Her plumpness graduated to obesity level one, the better to ground her as she sat stolidly, drinking her perfect Manhattan and making pronouncements; "I want prime rib tomorrow night."

Paula, built straight and thick as a tree trunk, Maddie's grounding fork, picked up the mantra and began suggesting restaurants. Susie, all lightness and air, bobbed her flaming red head, sipped the wine she liked to drink warm, and agreed.

Like lemmings who had brain surgery, the other six ladies in the group convinced themselves that prime rib was the thing, even if one was at the seashore for a week, near all those pesky lobster traps.

They were a carefully calibrated trio, whose sonar bounced effortlessly from one to the other, always knowing when to shift the power. If something was not going their way, then Susie, the frothy, likeable one stepped in to reinforce their wishes, and it was done like a knife slicing through warm butter.

Like the heavy brown and onion gravy that smothered the meat, the deeper intentions to criticize, rebuff, or be rude were often obscured by clever manipulation. This group think was facilitated by the genuine affection some of the women felt for each other, and so they would acquiesce to share a laugh or a kindness built on thirty years of friendship.

But, the witches were not about friendship. They threatened

Dee when she brought a woman who had never been accepted by them. Paula, her big tree trunk body blocking Dee, said, "That was a mistake." They were always rude to Patsy too and never accepting of her invitations to visit her little cottage here at the shore. Maddie, ensconced in a rocker on the porch of the inn she was staying at, upper lip still sticky from the breakfast maple syrup announced, "We're too busy," and heads nodded.

That morning Patsy, stunned by the rebuff that accelerated her heart beat, kept a plastered smile on her face, panicky to get away. She mumbled something like, "see ya," hopped on her bike and toodled off, her embarrassment fueling her pedaling legs. At home, she called her friend Cara who was no longer invited for the week of joviality. When Cara came she stayed with Patsy. She forewarned, "When the girls are down keep your distance."

Who would have thought the delicate balance of friendship that once ennobled and strengthened this group of diversified personalities would shift to an arena of petty hurts, power and manipulation. There were many times the celebration of their constancy was saluted, wine glasses held high, "Here's to us, still friends after all these years!

The witch's satellites, Jenny and Mavis, did their bidding even when their uneasiness could be seen in a shrug of the shoulder or a wandering glance. Words would be put to a lie. "It wasn't her idea," or "She never said that," dismissed an objection with a ferocity of flushed necks and deep sighs.

Then one summer, this summer, the stress began to fester as other voices refused to be squelched. "We're grown women, stop acting like sixteen year olds," said Dee. Patsy saw them once, then kept away and when people asked why she'd answer, "After seven years they have never even walked over here, I'm done being snubbed."

At dinner one evening, the ladies asked for separate checks, never done, never. Never done, for Maddie and Paula and Susie liked their apple martinis, warm wine, brandy and always had appetizers and huge, frothy desserts. They said, "We always split the check." Then Patsy spoke, "I'm an alcoholic and I ain't paying for your drinks."

Silence. "Me either, me either, me either." "I'm on social security." And so it went and so did they as they squeezed their buttocks, thigh to thigh into their car and drove off into the night.

### The Table

It sat in the middle of the room, a well-polished piece. Proudly it displayed delicately carved designs upon its sturdy frame. It was a table to behold, aged and scarred but beautiful and well-kept.

The room as she entered it smelled of wood and polish. The day outside was warm and lovely with the sounds of spring; birds chirping, their songs competing with traffic and human noises. They all intruded on the quietness of the room, which was bright with sunshine streaming through its windows. The sheer curtains let in every bit of buttery sun. It looked warm and homey, but Laura felt the underlying tension in the room. She knew the reason. She approached the table with trepidation, reaching out to touch its smooth surface. A shock went through her; electrical, painful. Surprised, she pulled away and retreated a few steps. Her body still thrilled with the tingle of the shock.

*Oh, yes, now I've got you,* she thought. *I knew it was you! I felt your presence in the antique shop. Finding you again took years, but you're finally in my hands.* Laura smiled. Not a pretty smile, more of a sneer. It wasn't an attractive face now, either; it didn't go with the shapely form that was attached to it. She was proud of her body, and flaunted it. And when she wore the pretty face with it, she turned many heads. Some showed envy, many-admiration. Laura Winston took full advantage of her looks, even though all she needed was to put a spell on whomever she pleased.

Laura was a witch; a real, spell-casting witch. Many years, centuries even, had perfected her skills; to get what she desired, whom she desired and be rid of them when they became boring. To all outward appearances she was an attractive redhead with the greenest emerald eyes and a complexion that any woman would die for. But a heart of blackest black beat within that comely body.

And Laura desired this table, for it held an old enemy within its wooden frame. The table knew her malicious nature and prepared itself for an unwelcome, vengeful attack. Despite the serenity of the room, a clash of wills between the two old foes was evident, but only to the foes themselves. Words not spoken were understood through thought.

She neared the table again, but it was ready for her. With a mighty shove it pushed her away. Grunting, Laura pounded on it, hurting her hand but knowing she hurt the table, too. "Welcome to my home. I have great things in store for you, none of which will be pleasant, I assure you."

*We'll see about that, bitch!* It countered.

Her plan was to have a dinner party upon this table for her many friends tonight. To show her old enemy that it was now in her power to belittle and demean it, she would use it for common purposes like meals and all the burdensome accouterments that went along with them. Oh, yes, she had planned it well.

Casting a temporary spell on the table, Laura held it in check while she threw an alabaster linen cloth over it. *You're suffocating me! Get it off!* Try as it might, the table couldn't dislodge the troublesome cloth, but merely managed to slide it to one side, until Laura put a pile of china on it to keep it still. "So my spell isn't as powerful on you, hmmm…? This is going to be a challenge, indeed." In time her best dinner service and silverware graced the table. The wonderful scent of roses filled the air as she placed the centerpiece, the final touch to the table. Yellow roses they were, to compliment the gold-trimmed china. Laura looked proudly at her work of art and commented, "You never looked so good, my dear." The table, in reaction, tried to knock things off its smooth finish, frustrated that it could only tremble. *Damn you, anyway; you'll be sorry!* She could almost feel the anger emanating from the helpless table, and she laughed as she left the room.

She hurried upstairs to get ready for the evening. As she dressed in front of the full-length mirror, Laura saw a beautiful woman, supposedly approaching her mid-thirties, though she could be any age she wanted to be; thick auburn hair framing those green seductive eyes and a full sensual mouth. *So…you spurned my love long ago; I'll bet you're sorry now,* she thought. *And now I have you where I want you.*

Laura dressed carefully, more for *it* than anything else. Her silver gray cocktail dress clung easily to her flawless body. Matching shoes complimented the dress. The icy cool diamond necklace and earrings completed the ensemble. As she poufed the two hundred dollar an ounce perfume around her, the room smelled like a garden of spring flowers. Again she glanced in the mirror for a final look. She looked stunning and she knew it. *I'll show him!*

The doorbell chimed; her guests had arrived. With a smile on her lovely face, she descended the stairway, looking forward to the evening.

As Laura entered the dining room with her visitors, there was a pleasant sense of welcome that pervaded the room. *Ah, so you've accepted your fate, have you?* She thought smugly. Chairs were drawn in noisily to the dining room table. Everyone was seated. She looked over her domain, secretly enjoying the seeming helplessness of the entrapped prisoner. Laura's guests clinked their crystal glasses in a toast to their hostess. As all hands touched, the room suddenly took on an air of evil. It shook with electricity; a blistering, scorching, all encompassing heat. Her hapless mortal friends were shuddering violently, arms and legs akimbo…THEY WERE BEING ELECTROCUTED!

And the dining room table shook, too…with laughter.

# *Groundhogs*

I said, I was running late. That's how I got my mother off the phone. Of course, I had to stop her in the middle of her Angela-bashing story. Angie is my newest sister in-law, struggling to find her place in the Stewart clan. I'm not quite sure what Mom was bashing about. I think she asked Angela to pick up some pumpkin seeds and beer on her way home. Angela forgot the pumpkin seeds which is certainly a reason to hate her guts. So now, Angie's a bitch, which is actually quite good for me. Now, I can come out of the dog house. There's another puppy waiting to take my place!

I hate when my mother calls me at 7 o'clock in the morning; like I have nothing better to do than to hear her daily dramas of pumpkin seeds and beer. She thinks because I don't work a nine to five job I must be sitting around every morning picking the wax out of my ears, waiting for some juicy tidbits. I guess to her graduate school *is* nothing – just an excuse not to grow up. Even though I told her I have nine a.m. classes to teach, complex experiments to run, theories to prove and lots of research papers to write, that didn't seem to impress her. In fact, one time she actually said, "maybe you should get a part time job; keep yourself busy."

My mother's recent fixation with my daily life started just after my last visit. It was the time she concluded I was having an affair. Her evidence: a short new haircut and a lost eight pounds. "Women only lose weight when they got a new lover," she said. Angie on the other hand had gained twelve pounds and started going the pony-tail route. Her marriage was on solid ground, despite her new dog house location.

But at least my mother saved me from the "*Dick Deliberations.*" They had just started. It's my least favorite time of the morning. It's when Richard will ask if I think his penis is too small. A subject that will just *happen* to come up because he thinks I was staring at it. And since, he's parading around nude, there's certainly nothing better to look at! He was *ironing*. Richard can't wear clothes when he's *ironing*!

THE DICK DELIBERATIONS

RICHARD:    Do you think my penis is too small?

CELIA:    No

RICHARD:    Are you sure?

CELIA:    Yes

RICHARD:    Do you ever wish it was bigger?

    (Celia desperately wants to get off the subject. She makes her answer more emphatic.)

CELIA:    Of course not!

RICHARD:    You know I never used to shower in the boys' gym. I was kind of embarrassed about my size.

CELIA:    Oh, really?

    (Richard begins a heart wrenching story about a young boy's inability to "measure up." The lights dim. The music fades.)

THE END

So, now I'm expected to restore him. A few hoops and hollers usually does the trick but this particular morning I wasn't in the mood! And I'll give Richard credit for this; he did *hip me* to the inter-workings of the male ego. I never knew that men hung around the showers comparing their "*stuff.*" I wanted to ask him, "do guys grab it and put them side by side?" Seeming that we women don't lay our tits out on the table and break out the rulers, I didn't know.

Now lately, he started putting a little twist to his act. A form of foreplay. At 6:45, he'll be prancing around the apartment with his robe wide open; his manhood, saluting the sun. He'll make a lot of noise, just to see if he can "*accidentally*" wake me up. Because if I'm already awake and he's not dressed, well then, we might as well…

But as I said, I wasn't in the mood!

Besides, I was right in the middle of one of my favorite fantasy dreams. The one where I go back in time and never get married. Instead, I keep dating Derrick and Brian at the same time. Boy, was that great! Derrick used to drive me around in his father's Mercedes and Brian wrote poetry – the good stuff! Shit you could understand! *What the hell was I thinking; marrying Richard? He didn't even meet my height requirement!*

Anyway, he made his final attempt to wake me up; opening the blinds, rustling hangers, unfolding the ironing board right next to the bed. Now in his mind, I can't possibly still be asleep because he's made enough noise to wake the dead. So he thought.

I stayed stiff as a rail, breathed really hard like I was nearly snoring and even let my mouth hang open wide. Someone once told me that when I'm sleeping real hard my mouth hangs open and I drool. I kept peeking through my lashes but I couldn't see him clearly. All I saw was his form. And his manhood.

Then, I guess he got frustrated that his plan wasn't working, he walked over to the bed and said, "hey." Now I knew if I opened my eyes completely, his penis would blind me on the left side. So, I acted groggy and I turned over on my stomach. I did everything I could to nicely send the hint: 'I'm still tired and I want to stay in bed.'

He touched my shoulder and gave me a nudge. I wanted to snap at him, but marriage laws say you can't just blurt out lines like, "*get the hell off of me! I'm busy dreaming about some old boyfriends and if you ain't one of them, you better go find some Vaseline or Wesson Oil.*" Personally, I think marriages would last much longer, if you could just say what's on your mind! Perhaps, it might've saved our marriage; but that's another story!

Well, thank goodness that was the precise moment my mother called.

He sprinted for the hallway phone, like he'd been caught or something. His manhood, slapping against his thigh, didn't seem to like the surprise, either. He coughed and cleared his throat, "Hello. Hey Sandy, how are you? Another day, another dollar. You know how it is."

On and on he went, sharing mundane morning pleasantries with my mother; crusty eyed, buck naked and his manhood slowly dying. If she only knew.

I got dressed immediately after she hung up. Richard made no progress himself; probably still living inside that pipe dream of pity-sex. My backpack was on my shoulder before he even zipped up his pants. He offered to drive me to campus but I preferred a quiet morning walk. Another day, another theory.

* * *

A warm and cozy sun beamed through tiny Venetian slits beckoning me to a joyous spring morning. I could feel the sun rays striped across my face. Shadyside's lone woodpecker mounted his daily assault on the young oak outside our window. *Who was he laughing at?* Me, I suppose; afraid to awaken in my own bed, trapped in a pretend slumber fearing nothing more than a "dangling" participle.

*I turned over on my stomach hearing the bathroom door close.*

His 40 minutes of shower, steam, herbal ointments and Caribbean roots, ended in the same heartbreaking phenomena as it had, time and time again. He was no bigger or stronger. His skin, no smoother; his hair, no fuller. His daily constitutional, no easier than before these daily rituals had begun. Life remained the same.

I heard the ironing board creak and rattle, well before it hit the bed. There was only a slight pause before the collection of metal and plastic hangers, clang and clattered; their excesses falling to the floor. He offered a loud and abrupt, "I'm sorry," just before the iron squealed out its burst of steam.

I peeked through my lashes watching him grab his faithful blue and baby blue "zipper pants." Swedish Knits was their actual name. A style that was all the rage in New York and far too cool to ever show up in the passé men's shops of Pittsburgh. They were an odd design. Solid colored pants with a waist to hem seam that ran down the sides. The seam was always in a bold and contrasting color, as if they were giant zippers. Once, a friend of his actually studied his hips, looking for the zipper pulls. Richard loved the style. He had six pair; green and olive, black and gray, gray and black, blue and maroon, brown and tan and his favorite, blue and baby blue.

It only took one steaming pass at the creases to realize he needed more light. He pulled the Venetian blinds in one fell swoop. Instantly, the sun, the birds, the lone woodpecker screamed their morning indictments; a new day, a new theory and I should be up and about.

I tempered my reaction, not jumping at the sudden burst of sun. I rolled over and snuggled my pillow tighter. "Oh, I'm sorry. Did I wake you?"

Jerk!

I didn't answer. I couldn't answer. *I was lost somewhere on Long Island, cruising Sunrise Highway in Derrick's father's brand new SL. We were laughing at the oddity; pulling up to the Burger King in an eighty thousand dollar car. We had sixteen dollars between us.*

I could feel the smile take over my sleeping face, so I buried it deeper into the pillow. Keeping my movements small, I breathed in and out driving my breath towards that dead-sleep sound. Richard returned to the closet, moving and shuffling hangers. A shirt? A sweater? *What the hell was he looking for?* A box from the shelf tilted forward and fell. A boom and crash. "Oh gosh! I'm so sorry Cele."

I peeked again. He was heading towards the bed, his penis in the lead. "Hey, you up? Sorry I'm making so much noise. What time is your first class?"

*What time was my first class?* The greatest come-on line in history! So if I'm not asleep and he's not dressed, well, then we might as well...

I'm damn sure not in the mood.

I jumped up looking towards the clock as if I'd overslept. "Oh wow!" It was five minutes to seven. "I've got a meeting with Dr. Simms at eight o'clock. I can't believe I almost forgot." I knew how to think fast on my feet. It took at least 15 minutes to get to campus. After a shower and my hair, there was absolutely no time to...

"Oh, you didn't mention that yesterday."

"Yea I almost forgot." I grabbed some underclothes from the drawer and headed to the bathroom. I thought I was safe, but I made one slight misstep. I glanced in his direction.

As if his nakedness was some mere accident, he pulls and adjust his robe. "Oh, wow," he chuckled. "Guess I should get dressed. You sure I'm not too small? I've always felt funny about letting others see my size."

"Yes, I'm sure." I quickly closed the door. Lifting the toilet lid was a clear sign for "no entry allowed." I could actually sense him outside the door, calculating, pondering how long his actual "ecstasy" would take. He finally concluded, there wasn't enough time.

\* \* \*

Early morning clouds soothed the beating sun. A soft gray light snuck through the tiny Venetian slits consenting to earth's request for a slower, quieter morning. I relished the thought that life was still a snooze button away, curling up tighter into the warm sheets. Richard didn't seem to understand the earth's request. He was moving abruptly, shoving draws and clanging toiletries. He sat on the edge of the bed to lotion his naked body. He sat on *my* side. He rubbed and smoothed as hard as he could. Bouncing and shaking the bed, like a ship at sea. I pulled the blankets closer to my chin and curled up. He said, "sorry."

I kept my eyes closed tight and pretended not to hear him. I felt him rub my leg through the blanket but I kept still, refusing to relinquish my sunrise fantasies. These quiet moments when reality didn't matter and my split worlds blended seamlessly. *Brian and I had commandeered a music room in Morrison Hall. He was playing the piano. Singing the words to a new composition; a poem he'd written for me years ago, now, a melodic rhythm. I blushed. I cried. This – was true foreplay!*

But the fullness of day soon invaded through fully drawn blinds. Metal hangers fell to the floor. The ironing board squeaked and rattled, as it hit the bed.

And I thought, "where the hell is my mother when you need her?"

# *The Unwanted Visitors*

He didn't bother to knock; he simply walked into the kitchen, eyeing the white-on-white room critically. "What was wrong with the yellow and gray?" he asked. "You didn't ask me if you could change anything." My father-in-law very seldom came up to the apartment. This visit was unexpected, but his overbearing attitude was not. The few times Joe Santos did dishonor us with his presence, he would open closet doors, look in drawers, in general be annoying and nosy. He wanted to see if anything was changed since he and his family had lived there. It was a huge apartment, a large kitchen, two bedrooms, one bath, a family room and a closed in porch. It was atop the cement block business that Joe owned. When his parents divorced, Tony's father moved his ex and kids to a house. When we married he was already living with his secretary. So here we were, which was great, for Tony was only making sixty dollars a week at the time.

I didn't answer him; it was done, what could he do about it? Granted it was his place, but we had done a nice job cleaning it up. His son, Tony, and I lived here. He was so controlling that we were told to ask permission to so much as hang a picture. He didn't seem to appreciate the fact that since we lived here, it made Tony caretaker. After hours people who came stealthily in the night to take products from the yard were foiled, for Tony always had an ear and eye out for thieves.

We didn't have much privacy because of our closeness to everything. If we could hear the men downstairs, they could certainly hear us. I learned more curse words and what men gossiped about from this vantage point; but the same was true for them. Nothing was sacred.

What was the point of this unwanted visit? I was sure I'd learn soon enough. And I did.

"Marge and Jack are going to move in with you. They're bringing the baby, too."

My jaw dropped. "What? But we're living here, we pay you rent. How can you do this to us?"

"It's my apartment; I can do anything I please. She's my daughter and I'm giving her a place to live." He said this smugly, almost with a sneer.

"But I'm pregnant, and there are only two bedrooms up here. The other is for the baby." I know I sounded whiny, but this idea was outrageous.

"She'll keep her kid in her room and you'll keep yours with you. You're damn fools for having kids now, anyway." What a bastard this man was! "I just wanted to give you a heads up, so you'll be prepared," he claimed. *Big Goddamned deal,* I thought. That smug attitude - I wanted to rip his head off. My hormones were doing strange things to me as it was- did I need this?

There was nothing spectacular about the man; average height, dark hair, very Italian. Joe was on his third wife and thought he was God's gift to women. You couldn't prove it by me, but then I never saw him with his pants down. Of course he had money, so the women put up with his old Guinea ways. He divorced Tony's mom to marry her best friend, killed his second, (well, she really died of cancer) and the third wife had it soft. Pun intended. Actually, I liked this last wife. She taught him manners and how to dress.

Tony gave him no back talk about the decision; he figured it was his father's place, it *was* his sister, and we had no money to live anywhere else.

Marge had a child at fifteen. Until she finished high school, her father boarded the baby with the nuns in the Trenton home for unwed mothers. Her parents both wanted her to give up the baby, but she refused. Good for her. She and I got along fine until now. I resented this turn of events. I didn't look forward to four adults and a two year old living here. Marge was childlike and spoiled. She was and is still a very pretty girl. But Sonny and I were only married for less than two years. We were still getting used to each other. I could already see what was coming- the lack of privacy, arguments about cooking, shopping, having friends over. I was really depressed.

I was *so* right. If we went shopping together, Marge got junk food while I bought the staples. She had young kids over and never cleaned up their messes. The baby peed on my new grey couch, causing a stain that never came out. Too late did I realize that maybe kids were a pain! The bigger my belly got, the more desperate I became to get rid of these interlopers.

One day, I went berzerk; grabbed a large kitchen knife and went into my sister-in-law's room, the one I wanted for my baby. I slashed at the walls, tearing the ugly rose-covered wallpaper into strips; and of course scaring the hell out of Marge. Here was this deranged, hugely pregnant woman, wielding a butcher knife. "Are you crazy?" she screamed. "You'll scare the baby!"

"This is supposed to be my baby's room," I screamed back at her. She ran crying to her father, who in turn figured his daughter-in-law was nuts, and got his little girl out of there. He set her up in a little place nearby, where the three of them didn't live happily ever after. They divorced after two years.

Things were peaceful in the old place again. I fixed up the baby's room and waited impatiently to lose the 65 pounds I had gained in my son's honor.

# The Togetherness Tango

*Surviving Retirement*

Just as the Christmas hype starts in October and makes most of us feel like inept failures for buying Pepperidge Farm stuffing and canned cranberries, the Retirement Lobby has created an image of perfect harmony in utopian settings. Silver haired handsome men and women in Lacoste shirts look adoringly at each other poolside, or at the club, or dancing on a twilight terrace. Yeah, sure. Just give me your first-born male heir and all this can be yours.

Perhaps some couples do find bliss in retirement, but I knew trouble was brewing the day Tom told me I was using the wrong mop on the hardwood floor. "It has residue on it," he said. Then, with a gleeful grin reminiscent of a four year old he emerged from the pantry with a blue handled mop displaying a tag that said, "wood floor." This was followed by a frantic leap to stop me from cleaning the microwave with Fantastic. "I wouldn't use that," he said, "It might explode."

I was not amused. This was just the beginning of the escalation of a domestic diva known as *the retired spouse*. I discovered a common thread with women in my cohort group, women who have work, friends, social engagements, volunteer activities, an occasional trip with pals, and a little mad money. As we raise our glasses to savor our long lasting friendships, laughing at the changes in our lives, ruminating on social security and Medicare, sooner or later the subject turns to our retired spouses and inevitably eyes will roll. "I think I'm going to kill him," is a popular theme.

The mystery we all ponder is, "How did these people run companies, make decisions, communicate, travel, become experts in something and are now focused on alphabetizing the soup cans?"

And while they were bossing people around in places like Sri Lanka or Kansas City we were fearless. We cooked. We cleaned. We painted. We wallpapered. We shopped. We kept the budget. We paid the bills. We went to ballgames. We were den mothers, class mothers. We took care of the car, the yard, the dog, the cat. We built things. We nurtured. We worked. We waited for Daddy to come home. Now Daddy's home, but he's waiting for Mom because she is usually out.

The other day I had three engagements. Tom was emptying the shredder. Emptying things is a favorite pastime, like the dishwasher. That is his job which makes me very grateful. He very carefully puts all the knives and forks in the right slot in the drawer.

It's as if all those organizational skills of the once busy man have been reassigned to finding just the right plunger for the toilet bowl. As I pondered this change of venue I discovered through anecdotal information there are common threads to the psyche of the retired gentlemen, one that requires an enormous adjustment on the part of us, the loving wives, one that is tooth gritting and stress inducing, one that requires a sense of humor and a good friend.

### *The Hormone Reversal*

A friend of mine with a penchant for wise remarks has said, "When did the hair on my vagina migrate to my chin?" We may be dehairing and sagging a bit, and we know why. Our estrogen has been replaced by progesterone, and my theory is that is why women as they age become more definite, involve themselves in activities they always wanted, cook and clean less, take their laugh lines and their elastic waist pants on a trip, or curl up with a juicy book and don't care if the dog needs to be walked.

Men, on the other hand, are losing their progesterone and begin to take on the attributes of their mothers. They become pantry and food focused. They love to go to places like Cosco and BJ's and buy enormous quantities of things like toilet paper, cat or dog food, paper towels, napkins, tomato sauce and soup, and they sort. Sorting is a big thing. Kitchen drawers, shelves, bookcases, all get the treatment. This often becomes an all day project. They clean. But, they only clean with special tools, like the hardwood floor mop. A picture cannot be hung until a hole is drilled into the wall with a special size bit before the ten pound specially weighted hanger is inserted. Ha, I say, there are still places in my home where lovely frames are gently balanced on pushpins.

### Multi-Tasking

Women are natural multi-taskers. We can whip through a house in no time, splash, sprit, fluff, and fold. We can pay our bills while the washer is spinning. We can scrub the bathroom while our hair color is tinting. We can hang a wallpaper border with an old sponge and a broken ruler. When we leave the house it is rarely for one reason, but to bank, market, go to the library, shop a little and the right side of our brain just keeps ticking.

Men can only do one thing at a time. If a man is balancing his checkbook do not interrupt for any reason. If a man is making a pot of coffee, do not go into the kitchen. If you, on the other hand, are about to watch the soap you haven't seen in a week and he wants to discuss the budget, a dirty look will convince him he is not appreciated. Let it go. Interrupting will get you nowhere anyway. "Dear, I smell smoke coming from the basement." "Oh, for Christ's sake, I'm balancing the checkbook."

Or, "I just need to get to the sink to take my life saving pills." "Okay, okay, I'll be out of your way in a minute. You didn't clean the drain."

### The Hoarding Instinct

We ladies are natural nesters. For me, a pleasant moment is sitting on a soft couch with a warm cup of hot chocolate in a "fluffed up" house, feeling the sun on my shoulders shining through a window.

Men collect stuff and order things on the Internet. Little treasures keep being delivered by UPS. The other day a set of speakers arrived. Absolutely no idea. We have a rug shampooer that takes up half a room. Thing is I have hardwood floors throughout the downstairs and carpeting in the bedroom. It is really overkill. We have a five disc interactive CD for the computer on how to speak Spanish. In the interests of storage efficiency we now have five plastic Christmas bins, one for balls, one for wreaths, one for left over wrapping paper, and two for the left overs. Now, mind you, these large, bulky red and green plastic things have shapes and compartments. The wreath storage is shaped exactly like a toilet bowl seat. The left over paper container is a long plastic cylinder that could be used to ward off an invasion of the Huns.

This is very different than nesting. They also bring things home from garage sales that they think will be just perfect for the hallway, the bathroom, the kitchen, and so forth. A dark pine Early American shelf with embellished corners does not blend well with my butcher-block black and white kitchen. My girlfriend's husband brought home an orange and brown area rug when they were redecorating their living room in pale lemon and soft green. He got it on sale and thought he was helping. The rug didn't stay.

They like to stay home. This is the biggest challenge to overcome, and there are creative ways that will help you not to grind your teeth. My husband can stay home for days on end, and when he does decide to venture out in the world it takes him hours before he finally leaves his nest. Today he said he was going to BJ's to stock up on coffee, toilet paper and cat food, and to look for a new chair for his desk. Okay, sounds good to me. I may actually have a few hours alone in the house. He leaves at 3 o'clock. By then I don't care. I've been watching the clock for five hours, tick tock, tick tock.

### Strategies to Stay Sane

My best strategy is to avoid conversation. This enables me to pretend he's somewhere else. The really good thing about this is that now he seems to sense when it is a non-speaking day. He gets the hint as I whirl through the house, mopping with the wrong mop, spritsing with the wrong chemical, nailing push pins into the wall, catching up on phone calls behind closed doors, or steaming my face in the dishwasher for a desperately needed skin rejuvenation.

Also, in lieu of locking myself in the bathroom, I just speak up. This is more difficult than one would think because retirement also brings extreme sensitivity to these guys, must be the hormones. I'll say, "I'm going upstairs and I need an hour alone." We then negotiate. Does he need to get his ratty work shoes from under the bed? Does he have a major project planned like sorting the paper clips into sizes and colors? Once the coast is clear I can then walk around covered in Nair with a mud mask on my face.

Keep doing what you like to do. Never, never, never get too drawn into his cycle of time management (which doesn't exist), depression (which does except it's only called a "mood"), and read the book "Co Dependent No More."

When you are feeling angry and irritable, call a girlfriend. She in turn will make you feel much better after you hear how Herbie brought home a case of chili and thirty cans of tomato sauce.

Last evening as we were enjoying a last of summer ice cream, he was taking forever to finish his sundae. I saw some friends across the room and said, "I'm just going to run over and say hi to Ginny and Jane." He gave me one of those sad, don't leave me here alone looks, but I went anyway. I chatted for a few minutes, then said, "Got to go, I can feel the invisible leash." They laughed and said, "Don't we know."

Then again, how can I be angry when he took it upon himself to get me a giant package of Depends on sale in BJ's. No idea, but the thought was nice.

## Blowout

The plane was descending.  We were on the last leg of another
vacation trip.  Coming home from South Carolina was always a letdown,
for Tony and I and our granddaughters enjoyed the condo on the beach.
We loved The Dunes, where we stayed each year, and the beautiful
weather.  I was feeling anxious, as I always did on taking off or landing.
It seemed like a normal descent; I could feel the landing gear emerging
from the bowels of the plane, and the slightly queasy sensation from
each level as we came down.  I looked around to see if anyone else was
concerned about these nervous moments before take off and landing.
Well, there were a few people who seemed on edge.  One youngster, eyes
squinched closed, sat white-knuckled in his seat.  A woman was loudly
saying her rosary; I knew *that* meant nervous! Most of the men sat
comfortably reading a newspaper or sleeping.  Tony himself was nodding
off.  The girls were sleeping soundly; they were used to traveling with us
and were old hands at it, even at two and four years old.

In a second or so we would all feel that first meeting of rubber
to pavement.  It was at that precise second all hell broke loose. The
plane was clearly out of control and the pilot was fighting to keep this
huge metal bird from destruction!  Wild-eyed, I looked around; the
oxygen masks had bounced down and were dancing like puppets in the
air.  Strips of aluminum siding on the plane had pulled off and were

falling onto the seats while we passengers were covering our heads for protection. While the plane careened all over the place, first left, then right, leaning one way then the other, the luggage began pouring from the overhead bins. (Later we learned that a tire had blown on touchdown, but that was later and this was now.)

Suddenly things seemed to be happening in slow motion. I became very calm, even though the plane was convulsing and we were all going to be battered to death by our own luggage!

Jaime, our two year old, was seated next to me, and across the aisle Tony had four year old Krissy. "Don't panic in front of the girls." I mouthed to him. It was hard not to however, for they were awakened by the screaming passengers and the jerking of the plane. Jaime, eyes big as saucers, grabbed me.

"Nonny, whatsa matter? I'm scared!"

"Don't worry, honey, it'll be okay. The plane is just being silly. I looked over at Krissy who was looking out the window.

"Make it stop, Pop-Pop, it's making me dizzy!" she cried.

Finally, with one loud squeal, the metal monster jerked to a halt. At that very second I happened to glance at the lady one aisle across from us. During the flight we had exchanged polite smiles, and she complimented us on how mannerly the children were. As I looked over at her the moment the plane bucked to a stop, something shot from her mouth- she lost her dentures!

In spite of the scary moments during the blowout, all I can think of when I think of that day is the poor lady's and my own surprised look when her false teeth popped out.

# *Style*

I suppose –
you write about
flowers and meadows;
laces and frills;
ancestral traditions that
warm your heart.

You speak of decades
and eras
and self made worlds,
the lifetimes you spent
cultivating grace.

An ancient
ivy
wraps your mind.
your memories are shaped
in
country colors.

And your words
reflect
this pastime search,
returning to a world
that loved you –
gentle.

Its sound is soft and
easy to hear.
I guess that's why
you speak it so
often.

Once,
I tried to speak
that way,
drawing a place
with endless skies.
I tried to mimic

your ancestral sound.

And  remember
you said –
"it's the same,
just,
different enough
to be me."

But when I spoke it,
in the country square.
no one knew its'
origin.

You said to me,
"speak it again,
this time, let them see the
colors."

But I knew
you were wrong.
they'd never see me –
I had no
country colors

So instead,
I write
epitaphs,
for my mothers' sons
and
daughters,
the way my mother
before me
had done.

It just took
a while
to plow your meadows,
to sew up the lace
and let the  flowers
die.

# Exodus

# It's Only a Number

Who is that woman in the mirror? I caught her quickly glancing at herself in the lingerie department of Macy's. She walked away, then, two steps back for another look, now leaning in, closer, fingers through her hair, tongue licking lipstick-gone lips.

She drops a package, a young salesman retrieves it, "here you go, Ma'am." Her back stiffens, she smiles, a very nice smile, her own teeth, but she can't get used to "Ma'am."

At first she didn't recognize herself when glancing quickly past a reflective surface, the snow-white hair, the jowls, that crepey old ladies neck. Well, hell, it took a long time, she thinks. Her eyes are dark, her hands have liver spots and freckles, but her nails are good. She puts a hand across her chest as if to check her grooming. Her new lace bra in hand, she heads for shoes, then sportswear. I saw her matching bright red high heels to a scarlet wool jacket. The salesperson said, "That color is stunning with your hair." She smiled. Today she treated herself with her first Social Security check.

# My Mother's Picture

He said to pick a picture that reflects who she really was, not just what I saw in her. But it's hard to look at any picture and not see the person I already know. How do you make a stranger out of years of confrontation? When I look, I still see a distant, demanding woman, who thought the world was ugly and cruel. But her portrait radiates beauty. Her lips, a perfect mauve are shaped like two joined crescent moons. They are slightly pouted, seeming to whisper some naughty word. Her head is tilted upwards in a delicate and regal pose.

She was not quite forty in the portrait, her face is trim and there are no obvious signs she is the mother of five. Her cheek bones are high, pulling the skin tight and gaunt – shaping her face with sculptured precision. And though her skin is deep dark, the color most of us dread, she wears it flawlessly, like a coating of chocolate dipped smooth and lucid.

Her eyes were lovely feline shapes, rounded in one corner and pointed toward the sky in the other. Luminous brown jewels that lure you near, but like two crystalline mirrors, you could see yourself inside them and never see a portion of her.

Her whispered brows, arched and defined, guide your eyes across

271

smooth temples. The lines of age and worry have not yet staked their place, though tiny gray streaks speak of days to come. Her hair is gently swept back, revealing the graceful form of her face.

There is nothing that I inherited from her graceful beauty. Her slender neck and petite chin seem to be her own personal blessing of ancestry. She wasn't very tall, but her slim legs and tiny waist made her appear much taller and statuesque. She wore her long wavy hair, twisted and elegantly pinned. It was a dark muted auburn color, often called sandy brown. And thus, the reason they called a bold and daring woman, appropriately named Ruth, by the obscure, unsuited nickname, "Sandy."

* * *

Since her hair had completely grayed, I would not let them bury her with the name Sandy. Beneath her pale and wrinkled skin, I could still see her rich deep color. The woman named Ruth had lost her petite figure, her eyes had clouded and her lips seemed only to cry in pain. But in honor of the graceful and majestic beauty I'd always known, and the proud woman she'd forced me to become, I closed the casket and displayed this picture.

# *In a Lifetime*

are you still allowed to
call yourself an orphan,
even
though you're old enough to walk,
or run, or fly, or
fight, or kill, or maim, or die

of loneliness, or win,
or lose, or lose your way,
or lose your money and lose your home,
or lose your right to say

yes or no,
or lose control and lose your mind,
or find a man and
then
lose control and lose your mind,

or hide and seek,
or buy, or sell your soul,
then sell your heart and live in hell,

or lie, or cheat, or be afraid,
or lie about
the life you made and then

pray to God you don't die alone,
or die before you've had the
chance to live and
leave behind
your only chance to love?

### ❦

# *Getting Older*

I lie in bed, not wanting to get up yet. The sun slants through the metal blinds, disturbing my need to stay in darkness awhile longer. Snug in the warm comfort of the covers I glance around the room. Today the cool white and mint green walls don't seem as cheerful as they usually do. On the window sill a black and yellow finch chatters to its mate, a bright chirping call, but even that doesn't touch my heart. Today is my 70th birthday. *But how can I be seventy when I still feel sixteen; okay, maybe twenty.*

Tony claims that he can't tell if I've gotten older; he still sees the 16 year old when he looks at me. *Of course, at our age the eyesight dims-maybe that's a good thing.* Tony's the gray-haired man who lives with me in this house we built together. He's the man who went from a 34 inch waist to a forty; my fault, he says, for being a good cook. He's the man who wears my 18 inch belt around his Stetson hat; and the man who put up with me for 52 years. The stubborn, hard-working guy who loves me despite the fact that I now have *his* old waistline! He's the same boy who finally fell in love with the young pony-tailed girl who loved him the minute she laid eyes on him. At the tender age of eleven I knew he would be mine.

To this day, I remember that age of indecision-the teen years. Will other girls like me? Will a boy ever want me? What happens after

275

graduation?  A cemetery of memories are unearthed; being in the school choir, getting A's, weekend parties, the beach in the summer.  On the other hand, playing hooky and getting expelled a gazillion times.  Feeling bad, too, that my parents never came to my school functions; the musical programs, the plays, or the parents' nights.  In all fairness, Daddy was away a lot, and Mom worked the 3 to 11 shift at Bendix.  Still…

Finally, with a sigh of resignation, I swing my legs to the side of the bed, grunting as I sit up.  Standing, I adjust my silky pink nightgown, shimmying to bring it down from where it worked its way up to my waist during the night.  I admire the piece of fluff; I like pretty things.  Outwardly, though, I dress carefully casual, never tucking blouses in, not with the middle bulge I'm carrying around lately.  *But these days I'm more content with my looks than I have been in a long time.  I know I'll never be tall or thin or look like Sophia Loren.*

I pad to the bathroom to do the routine morning ablutions; Pee, wipe, flush and stand, only to come face to face with the dreaded mirror.  *My skin doesn't fit me well anymore.  But the failing eyesight blessedly forgives the cellulite around my thighs and belly.  And I need to firm up the flying squirrel flaps I call my upper arms.  Maybe I should have thought of that a long time ago.  Too late!*

Wide awake now I walk to the kitchen, wriggling my toes happily on the shaded blue tiles.  I hate shoes, hate my size nine feet.  With a nostalgic sigh I remember my mother trying to pacify me when I was young and complaining about them.  She'd say, "Big feet, lotta knowledge." I smile at the memory and realize that I'm whistling.  I'm not upset anymore, about my birthday or anything else.  I putter around the kitchen I love; the bright skylight over the sink, the oak cabinets, the royal blue countertop.  They're all conducive to getting me out of a gloomy mood.  This is my favorite room in the house.  No matter who comes to our home, they always end up in the kitchen.  *Even if the president came to visit he'd have to sit in the kitchen like everyone else.*

*Like my writing group that meets here every week- in the kitchen, of course.  There's Patsy, Celia, Rick, Pat and Vicky.  We all met at a local college creative writing class, and kept it going when the classes were over.  I was in my 60's at the time.  Taking those courses was one of the best things I ever did-I love writing!  The group's feedback keeps me motivated.*  I began writing and illustrating a children's book, and with the encouragement of the others, especially the patient help of Patsy, I published it. *What a great feeling!*

  *So I'm a late bloomer- and I'm still learning! Yes, next year I'll have even more wrinkles, but...every wrinkle has a story.*

  I shower, dress, and leave the house, which could certainly use a vacuuming, and go off to meet Patsy for lunch.

# *Reunion*

The March wind rattles off the ocean shaking the windows of
the house, and I feel the chill. It is the fiftieth reunion of my high school
graduation at Dominican Commercial and I've been found. I will go
to this rite of passage, this cleansing of the past, this curious journey to
nowhere and everywhere. My head is now covered in a towel as steam
rises up from the boiling water. I am giving myself a facial, trying to
cleanse and tighten the pores on my sixty seven year old skin. This
occasion requires serious plucking, pruning and soothing. As I lift the
dreaded magnifying mirror to my face I am sixteen again, agonizing over
pimples and a bad perm, dabbing flesh colored Clearasil on my face. I
lather cream on those tiny lines around my mouth.

I am going to Dominican Village for the reunion luncheon, the
name itself conjuring hordes of bright young women in a trauma ward
of respectability and fear. It is where the elderly nuns live, the nuns
who once wore pristine white gowns and black and white wimples, their
long black wooden rosary beads swinging as they walked, their mission
unwavering, to enrich our brains and capture our souls. When I told
friends I was going to Amityville, they said, "I hope it's not haunted," but,
of course, it is.

I dig out old photos tucked in a weathered album, secured neatly
with tiny black triangles in each corner. I see a jumble of bodies in a bed

at a sleepover, all arms and legs and laughter. I see girls in tulle prom gowns, shyly standing arm in arm with young and unsure men in tuxedos. I see me with Rosalie in similar checked Easter coats, absurd flowered hats on our head, and Louise and me bundled up in winter coats, look alikes, tall and Irish. I see Mary, my once best friend, heads together smiling broadly at a birthday party.

And I wonder why I am doing this, why I am returning to a time when my life began to swerve away from its core, like a great abyss claiming another girl victim, a victim of a crisp and proper decade devoted to propriety, a decade so docile that Elvis Presley's hips shook the country more than the A-Bomb scare. It was a time when my adolescent angst believed that I was born one second too early or one second to late, cursed to march behind the Pied Piper of conformity, my spirit squelched by the invisible giant girdle of patriarchy that squeezed out the juice of blossoming women buds.

It was all so long ago. It was the Age of Virginity. It was an itchy, brown wool uniform and Dominican Nuns. It was about finding a nice little job, and a nice beau or joining a convent. It was not about freedom. The beat of my internal drummer was numbed, but its soft beat tickled, teased, leading me away from the early marriage, the nest, the expected.

But, the sisters had trained me well for my first job in my eighteenth summer. Downtown Manhattan with its narrow angled streets clinging to high office buildings was a friendly neighborhood injected with enormous energy. I can still feel the rhythm of Liberty Street and Maiden Lane, the quiet space of Trinity Church, the wide expanse of Broadway, the green at Battery Park, the hustle, the warmth, the buzz.

* * *

*What little brown birds we were huddled together at the bus stop.* No competition to the girls in pink angora sweaters, full poodle skirts, pushed up breasts in pointy bras who went to Richmond Hill, the public high school. Me, Mary, Louise huddled at the bus stop, eyes downcast, fearful of a derisive comment from some nasty boy. But not Katie. No, she was to be envied, her five foot two inch frame generously endowed, her breasts filling the saggy droop of her uniform.

A favorite with the nuns, she starred in all the musicals and although she always sang off key her renown as a great stage presence never diminished. Oh, my God, those shows! Like a reverse Hasty Pudding Club the annual musical was cast with tall or fat girls as boys, Katie a countess or a princess.

Ballroom dancing was required of all proper ladies. Louise and I, tall and skinny learned how to lead, hands properly positioned just so on the shoulders and waists of our shorter partners. We could fox trot, rumba, waltz and tango and unlike Ginger Rogers never learned to dance backwards. My husband still tells me to stop leading.

Now I am on my way to Long Island, up the Garden State Parkway, the New Jersey Turnpike, the Verrazano Bridge. I zip by in the HOV lane on the Long Island Expressway at eighty miles an hour, my grip tight on the wheel. I am hooking up with Rosalie, the old pal who found me. We were together in Miami Beach, the summer I turned twenty-one. She met her first husband Joe that week, his intensity of love, masking the manic depression that eventually destroyed their marriage. We kept in touch in the early years, and then the chasm widened, perhaps when my alcoholism claimed me and the trauma of her divorce consumed her. She opens the door and we look at each other in soft focus that melts the years, and the easy and comfortable rapport we shared chips away at the iceberg of time. Rosalie opens the fridge and takes out a bottle of port wine. She says, "I thought we'd have a glass of port to toast your Mom. I loved your Mom. She'd always give us a glass of port and sat with us after we came home from one of those horrible dances." And there it is. But I am okay. I have prepared for the inevitability of wine and good cheer for I know that my disease is death with one quick motion of the elbow, hand on glass. I tell her "I am an alcoholic." She flutters her hands, returns the wine to the fridge. I tell her it's okay, and the moment passes.

Soon we are on our way to Dominican Village. A gray haired woman in a navy blue polyester blazer waves us off to a second parking lot and Rosalie says, "I bet she's a nun. Has to give orders." The lobby is crowded with women in fashionable slacks and jackets, flashes of color and bling invigorating the atmosphere. I find my badge with my high school graduation picture and name. As I make my way into the dining hall I am hit with a tsunami of long lost girls. The girls from grammar school and Glendale, the crowd of sleepovers and crushes and summer dances in Forest Park, the girls whose parents gathered at the Glendale Catholic Club, who let us have highballs on occasions and parties in the basement. Peggy and Evelyn and Terry and Louise. "Oh, my God, I'd recognize you anywhere." And they point to my dark brown almost black eyes and say, "Your smile. You always smiled with your eyes."

Someone says, "Have you seen Mary?" It would surprise anyone to know how we lost touch, went our separate ways for after all we were best friends at six years old, wending our way through grammer school and then Dominican. I led her down the aisle on her wedding day, maid of honor in a red velvet gown with a soft circlet of white fur on my long brown hair. She only wanted Joe, a seminarian she scooped out of a life of celibacy, a young man who came home with her brother who is still a priest. And so, off she went and I rarely saw her after the wedding, and then not at all. And here, nearly fifty years later I'm still tender.

She comes toward me, her face fuller, her hair like mine, short and white. We hug. Peggy says, "I have to get a picture of you and Mary together." We pose. I feel nothing. I only see a lovely sixty seven year old woman I once knew as a little girl, a teenager, and then a bride.

Rosalie hails me from across the room and we sit down for lunch and chatter. Yearbooks are passed and raffles are sold to benefit the nuns. I spend some time with Louise who tells me she married a Jew which was enormously brave for an Irish Catholic from Dominican. She too, says her husband accuses her of leading. I see a pack of Marlboros peeking out of her purse. Conspiratorially I say, "Want to go outside for a smoke?" We stand outside puffing away, checking in our rear view eyes for nuns, sixteen and sassy again for a split second in time.

# A Piece of Nature

The falling leaves
   float slowly to the ground
And lie in piles
   in every road and gulch
Their colors melt
   in wait for next year's mulch....biding their time.

A gusty wind blows
   thro' the balding trees
Making them bow
   like courtly gentlemen
Ruffling the feathers
   of each little wren....that lives in there.

The bare land shivers
   fearing winter's cold
In wait for snow-
   that pristine powder of white
To cover all,
   knowing that Spring's light...will warm its world.

# The Change

I awake in a puddle, I'm drowning in sweat.
Women don't sweat, friends say-did you forget?
Oh, yeah, I heard that one a long time ago
Horses sweat, men perspire, but women 'glow.'
Bullshit! Say I- when you get so wet
That you must change nightclothes and linens- that's sweat!
My doctors are male; they don't believe-
You're too young, they tell me-I sit and grieve.
A spiteful thought fills me with so much elation
I'd love them to drown in their own perspiration!
For they'll never know that particular flush
That makes your hair stick to your scalp from that rush
Or feel the trickle between their breasts
While they're dining out with important guests.
The river runs down your spine as you squirm in your seat
You don't feel so great-you turn red as a beet.
In winter when everyone's freezing their asses
A hot flush begins and fogs up your glasses.
Normal folks bundle up and just go
I want to strip and roll in the snow.
By now we know Change of Life was the reason
That I flushed hot, no matter the season.
A hysterectomy solved it-there's no more downpour
It's comforting to know I don't 'glow' anymore.

# *Friendship*

You unfurl
    A delicate ribbon
Curling, twisting, wrapping me in
    your soft silken embrace, or
Knotting and ripping in waves
    of distrust, anger, carelessness

Your fiber strings of heart so tender
    fill my sorrow for ills beyond repair
Both taken and given on roads
    of broken stone

Deep the ways your winding paths
    beckon, guide, embrace
My journey through the mist of life
    me to you and you to me
Where eyes and smiles cajole the dark and
    light the night of memory

Forgiveness whispers
    leaving gratitude
For friendship old and gnarled
    the twisted limbs of years well spent
Where ageing faces speak of beauty
    once remembered as the silent night
        of life arrives.

Printed in the United States
209975BV00001BA/220-318/P